Bat Valley

and Other
Strange African Animal Stories

Robert Gurney

ISBN 978-1-9997416-0-0
Copyright ©2017 Robert Gurney

Published by
Llyfrau Cambria Books, Wales, United Kingdom.
*Cambria Books is a division of
Cambria Publishing.*
Discover our other books at: www.cambriabooks.co.uk

Cover design by William Gurney

Acknowledgements

I would like to thank once again Dr Clive Mann for his tremendous help with this book. His advice has proved invaluable. He has provided on far more than one occasion inspiration for parts of these stories.

The Stories

INTRODUCTION

The first story, *'The Okello's Camper Van Man'*, tells the poignant tale of a dying Englishman kept alive by an abandoned Ugandan orphan.

The second, *'The Gecko Man of Lugard's Fort'*, explores the relationship between an English academic who has fallen on hard times in Uganda and the Tutsi refugee who cares for him.

'The Old Man and The Stride' is a dialogue between a visiting academic and a strange local gentleman. It takes place in a park in Kampala in front of a statue that represents the future of the Commonwealth.

'The Buffalo Men of Akagera' describes the relationship between an American, part First Nation, and an Englishman. It describes their common interest, the buffalo, and their violent end.

'The Beautiful Butterfly People of Kanyawara' reports on a comic academic conference, financed by the European Union, held at Bat Valley University in Kampala.

The protagonist in *'The Chameleon of Buntuntumula'* experiences an illumination one day on coming face to face with a chameleon. As a result, he develops a new theory of education for a developing nation, one that gets him into some trouble.

'The Chicken Man of Mbarara' describes the trials and tribulations, the frustrations and failures that beset an African American intent on returning to the land of his fathers.

'The Crane Lady of Mperwerwe' follows the adventures of an eccentric young Englishwoman who gets carried away by her research and forms a strange relationship with a Crested Crane.

'The Crocodilophile of Mukusa Island' traces the progress of a man's obsession with crocodiles, one that lands him in trouble with the law.

'The Herpetologist of Nabajuzzi Swamp' is the sad story of a man so obsessed with frogs he becomes totally isolated from

other human beings.

'*The Gorilla Man of Bwindi*' is a cautionary tale in which the reader is asked to contemplate the fate of a man who attempts to swindle a charity out of money in order to fulfil an African dream.

'*The Gower Hippo Boy*' accompanies a Welsh academic, as he travels down the Nile researching hippopotami, eventually meeting his maker, trampled to death, on the shores of Lake Victoria.

The object of desire at the heart of '*The Jaguar Men of Kiziba*' is the last King of Rwanda's Jaguar Mk5 coupé. Based on a true story, it includes Princess Margaret's state visit to Uganda. The main character's weakness, envy, leads to a dramatic ending.

'*The Lungfish Man of Mbazi*' has a relatively happy dénouement. It involves a research programme at Bat Valley linked to space exploration that almost ends in disaster for the researcher.

'*The Mount Elgon Waiter*' culminates, in a Fawlty Towers-like scene in a tourist hotel, in a reference to witchcraft.

'*The Moth Lady of Tororo*' finds an ageing British lawyer almost falling for a glamorous young post-grad student in a swimming pool situated in a hotel near the Uganda-Kenya border.

'*The Kampala Shopping Mall Ostrich Man*' examines the disgraceful behaviour of a married Lothario.

'*The Owl Man of Mukuno*' is a dark tale involving an Englishman, his Mugandan wife and his mother-in-law.

'*The Bat Valley University Praying Mantis Man*' delves deeply into a work by the surrealist artist M.C. Escher: 'Dream'.

'*The Snake Lady of Nakasero*' involves a man's deep fear of snakes, his efforts to overcome it, a doomed relationship and a fatal snakebite suffered during curfew.

A fear of spiders is the subject of '*The Spider Man of Gulu*'. It features the spoiled daughter of a member of the British Establishment who overcomes her fear only to meet an unexpected end in the north of Uganda.

'The Congolese Warthog Man' relates how a man from Katanga, turning his back on the ivory trade, learns how to love a warthog.

Finally, 'Bat Valley' tells the story of a man whose all-consuming interest in bats leads to near-disaster.

The Okello's Camper Van Man

Cecil lived in a large camper van behind Okello's Bar. Okello was a good sort. He allowed people who were passing through to use his small, bare-earth car park. Cecil had been there for a quite a while. His health was failing. Okello did not have the time to look after him properly. His business was not doing too well. He had to work as a security guard after his bar shut at midnight. The bar was failing.

Little by little things deteriorated. The van's tyres went flat. Cecil was unable to inflate them. As his health declined, he realised that he would no longer be able to drive. The rotting van became a permanent fixture.

Nsubuga was homeless. He was a kind child. Aged nine, he fended for himself. He had no idea where his parents were. Some said they were dead, victims of one of the waves of violence that had swept through the country. He had learned how to survive. There were rich pickings to be had in Kampala.

One day he knocked on the door of Cecil's van. Cecil called out weakly that the door was never locked.

"Can I help you, sir?" Nsubuga asked.

"I am all right, young man," Cecil replied.

Nsubuga could see that he clearly was not. He fetched some water from a tap behind Okello's bar. Cecil drank it greedily.

"You need looking after, sir."

Cecil did not put up a struggle. He knew the child was right. Nsubuga began to see how much needed to be done. He opened a fridge that a friend of Okello's had donated. It was heaving with cockroaches. There were cockroaches everywhere, on the floor, on the walls. The side of the van behind the fridge appeared to be moving: cockroaches. As he moved around the van, it sounded as if he were walking on potato crisps.

4

"What have you been eating?" he asked Cecil. Cecil did not reply.

"The fridge is empty, sir, apart from the cockroaches."

It dawned on him: Cecil had been surviving on cockroaches.

"Sir!"

"They are full of nutrients, my son. You can live on them."

Nsubuga settled in. He had nowhere else to go. He made a small bed for himself in the roof of the converted van. The Luton van has a space above the driver's seat. It became his home.

He set about building Cecil up, sharing whatever food he could lay his hands on. When the giant grasshoppers, the *nsenene,* came flying into town, he would borrow a sheet from the van and erect it somehow under a street light near the City Bar. Drawn by the light, the insects would collide with the sheet and slide down. On a good day, he could fill a plastic carrier bag. He would take them back to Okello's yard and fry them with a bit of onion on a wood fire by the van. Cecil loved to eat them with a little salt. He loved the aroma they gave off as they were being fried.

Nsubuga knew of many places in Kampala where there were termite hills. He would sit patiently by the heaps on Kitante Hill, for example, prodding the insects out. He knew the exact time of the year when the reproductive adults came out in their millions. These too would be fried or grilled on the little fire by the camper.

Cecil began to put on some weight but he was still in a bad way. Nusbuga was not going to be defeated. He had found a home. He no longer had to sleep under bushes in the park in the city centre.

"I will bring you something nice tonight," he told Cecil.

It was Tuesday. Tuesday was 'hotels day'. Little Nsubuga had a weekly programme. Wednesdays were the bins behind the halls of residence at Bat Valley University, Thursdays the skips behind supermarkets and Fridays involved waiting patiently for half-eaten burgers to be discarded by students celebrating the end of the week in Wandegaya.

Cecil began to regain not exactly a zest for life but at least the will to survive. Nsubuga would bring him half-empty bottles of Coca Cola. These were a real treat.

Cecil's new-found friend began to devise even better plans. He noticed that Cecil had some nice clothes in the van. With his host's approval he took these down to Lowino Market where he would get a good price for best quality cashmere sweaters.

Cecil was essentially bed-bound. He could not go out, unless Nsubuga could locate a wheel-chair and that was an impossibility. If only he could ease Cecil out onto the back edge of the van so that they could enjoy an *al fresco* barbecue, that would be tremendous.

Back in the city - Okello's bar was on the outskirts – Nsubuga set about rummaging around in hotel refuse bins. He would hang over the edge of the bins, and dip his hands deep into the rubbish within. His aim was to find silver spoons. On a good day he could retrieve three or four, each with the coat of arms or the name of the hotel engraved on it. They fetched good money at the market. Cecil's diet improved.

Meanwhile, back in the van, the cockroach problem was coming under control. They had not gone away but there were far fewer of them. Things were improving by leaps and bounds.

Nsubuga discovered that the chefs in the kitchens of the student canteens at Bat Valley would often throw out unused *matoke*. Mounds of the banana mash were prepared each day to go with the stringy meat served up to students. He explained that he was looking after a former lecturer in English at the university. The chefs knew that he was telling the truth. A number of lecturers who had "stayed on" had fallen on hard times. Their pensions had dried up. Deep down, the chefs knew that they had to help. They remembered Cecil. He had cut an unusual figure when he arrived unannounced and uninvited at the university. He had managed to get some strings pulled in Oxford and Bat Valley and had been offered a lectureship but without a proper contract.

On some days Nsubuga would arrive back at the van with a bag full of bananas handed to him by the chefs. He would scoop out a depression in the earth, peel the bananas, wrap them in banana leaves – there were several banana trees in the parking area - and place them in the hole, over which he would place wood. Cecil would watch from the back of the van while the bananas cooked in the hot ashes under the fire.

Climbing up onto a skip behind the IT department at Bat Valley, Nsubuga noticed something sticking out. It was an old computer, an early laptop, complete with charger. He retrieved it and took it back to Cecil. Cecil was delighted when he discovered that it worked. Okello allowed him to run a cable from the bar to provide electricity for the charger. Cecil was returning to the world.

Out of the blue one afternoon, his estranged wife dropped in to visit. She was on her way to East London in South Africa. She and Cecil had bought a bungalow there for their retirement but their marriage had broken down. She was shocked at the conditions in which her husband was living. She set about restoring some order. Nsubuga was annoyed because he thought things were fine but he bit his tongue and said nothing.

Cecil and his wife's separation had been acrimonious but Cecil hoped all that was water under the bridge. He asked Okello if Nsubuga could sleep in the bar for a while. Rosamund moved up into the tiny "upstairs bedroom" in the van.

She was sitting with him inside the van having breakfast. Things, at that moment, were calm between them. She had been going on about the cockroaches but, otherwise, they seemed to be getting on reasonably well.

Now, Nsubuga would often bring home a bundle of old newspapers that had been thrown out behind the Imperial Hotel. He would wrap himself and Cecil up in these on cold nights.

"Pass me that newspaper," she said.

Cecil had already been put out by some of his wife's

comments about his life-style, but he had kept quiet. For some reason his irritation suddenly came to the surface.

"You are really backward, Rose. Don't you know the world has moved on? Here, use my laptop."

Looking down, she saw a cockroach scuttling away from the van. She jumped out and stamped on it. It kept on moving.

"What did you say?" she asked angrily.

"Don't you have laptops in South Africa? Here, you can catch up with the news with mine."

Furious at his comment, she took the laptop and threw it at the cockroach that she had just tried to kill. It carried on running. The insides of the computer spilled out onto the earth.

The following day. Nsubuga moved back into his bunk and Rosamund continued on her journey south.

The Gecko Man of Lugard's Fort

It's difficult to know where to start. I could start at the beginning but that would take too long. I'll start with the here and now.

I am lying in bed. I can hardly move. My faithful friend Jean Bosco brings me my food and attends to my needs. He has been with me on Nakasero Hill since 1965. I bought the flat from a soldier at a time when everything was up in the air in Uganda.

Jean Bosco doesn't live in the flat. He lives out the back in a concrete building that he has occupied since he came to work for me. He works at the French Embassy now as a chef. Sometimes he can only call in to see me once a day.

I spend most of my day staring at four walls. Of course, I have not always been like this. It came on slowly. Little by little I have become incapable of movement. Now I am bed-ridden.

You might say I am unlucky. I am not. I still have my friends. You see, my work, before I fell ill, involved lecturing and research at Bat Valley University. My research there was on geckos. We were trying to form a new research centre dedicated to the study of the ways in which the little creatures could assist humankind.

When I arrived, I was working closely with a young lady who was studying the ears that grasshoppers have on their knees. I was never bold enough to ask her how having ears on one's knees could be of use to Humanity.

The thing that fired my imagination was the way geckos could walk on walls and on the ceiling. I first noticed them in the washrooms at Bat Valley. They seemed to like the dampness in there, as well as the peace and quiet. I would stare at them when I was shaving. There were no windows in there, only the electric light. This created a strange, other-worldly atmosphere.

9

One evening I went to have a wash and there was a bat 'looking up' at me from the concrete floor. That could have been a seminal moment for me. Strange atavistic sensations ran up and down my spine. But no, it was a one-off experience. The geckos were there every day. They were my constant companions.

I proposed to my professor that we should launch a project studying geckos' feet. At first I thought he was going to turn the idea down. He was heavily involved at the time in studying how chameleons change colour. His work had attracted funds from international pharmaceutical and beauty products firms, as well as grants from American private hospitals. He had published articles in a number of neuroscience journals.

I thought he would turn my proposal down, on the grounds, unacknowledged of course, by him, that it would be too close to his area, that I would be, to all intents and purposes, a rival. There is a lot of that sort of thing in the academic world. In the event, he was delighted with my idea. I managed to get him on board by suggesting that he add his name to mine on future academic papers that I wrote. He controlled the purse strings, you see.

That is how it all started. My first paper was about the way geckos' feet cannot stick to Teflon. I argued that Teflon had been engineered to resist the Van der Waals force. This paper attracted plaudits from around the world.

Eventually my research caught the eye of NASA scientists, who saw immediately a possible application. My discoveries, if they proved to be convertible into man-made substances, could revolutionise space travel. Spacemen and women would be able to walk on the ceilings of their space ships, not on Teflon, of course.

I managed to land a huge grant from Hollywood. An entrepreneurial film-maker saw in my research a way of cutting back on expenses when making Spiderman films. Large New York cleaning firms began to look into my idea for boots that would allow, for example, a window-cleaner to walk up the side of a sky-scraper. Special operations experts came to Kampala to see if my discoveries could be used by teams of Navy Seals boarding pirate ships.

All that is in the past. Here I am now, sick and alone. Can I create Art Gecko whilst in bed, I ask myself? I have tried but it's physically difficult. I am alone, except, that is, for my little friends, the geckos.

I managed to get my collections of geckos brought up to my flat. Jean Bosco eases me into my wheel chair now and then so that I can go from room to room to say hello to my companions. Most of them live in vivaria dotted around the flat.

It is a strange flat. I don't know exactly when the block was built, somewhere between the two world wars, I imagine. It has large cavernous, echoing rooms. It is dark inside. The windows are covered with a fine mesh to stop mosquitoes getting in. They get in anyway.

When I first moved in here in the nineteen-sixties, I would spend half an hour each night throwing a pillow at the mosquitoes on my bedroom wall. The nightly tally was at least half a dozen, sometimes more. The trick was to throw the pillow at a point just in front of the insect. 'Mozzies' tend to jump forward when they take off, presumably to avoid the lash of the sticky long tongues of chameleons and geckos. I observed that geckos often just use their jaws to snap up their prey.

Little by little the wall of my bedroom became a mass of blood from the squashed insects. Whose blood was it? It was impossible to know. Presumably it belonged to people lower down the hill. I once toyed with the idea of initiating a research project, examining the blood inside mosquitoes and comparing it with samples taken from people living further down. I decided against it when I heard that the dictator lived in a street somewhere below my window. Was that his blood on the wall, I wondered? I dismissed the idea as ridiculous. The project never got off the ground.

So here I am, by myself, with only geckos to keep me company. They do the work now of removing the mosquitoes.

For that small mercy I am mightily thankful.

They are plucky little blighters. I bought a tall second-hand fridge. It turned out to be infested with cockroaches. My geckos would take them on, locking their jaws around the foul creatures' heads, creating a cracking noise as they did so.

I am not totally inactive. Jean Bosco is very good to me. He spoils me, as much as he can. I cannot pay him anything now. He has stuck by me through thick and thin. He fled from Rwanda and says my door was the first he knocked on in Kampala. He doesn't have to live where he does, behind the flat. His wife, who has some aches and pains, would be more comfortable in the premises the French Embassy offers its staff. That's how he is, though, loyal to a fault.

The university pays my council tax and has provided me with a pension that is just big enough to cover the food Jean Bosco buys for me in the African market. The fillet steak he gets hold of is as good as any sold in the city's top supermarkets.

Jean is getting weak himself now. His hair is silver, as is his goatee beard. Nevertheless, he will go out of his way to assist (some say to humour) me. He has helped me set up a small research experiment in my room. Combing the stalls of Lowino outdoor market, he has come up with tape recorders, loudspeakers and microphones.

Which brings me to my project. The thing that astonishes me about myself, when I was fit, is that I paid so little attention to the sounds geckos make. In fact, I have to confess that for a long time I was practically unaware of their sounds. This is partly because Bat Valley University, despite appearances, can actually be a fairly noisy place, both during the day and at night. At night there is a whole symphony of sound in the air, created by a variety of creatures.

Lying here in bed one day, I realised that I was finding it difficult to describe the sounds that geckos emit. The flat is a quiet place owing to its distance from the noise of traffic in the valley below. I have become hypervigilant, you could say, to small noises in the night. This may go back to the time of disorder in the seventies, when, armed with machine guns, gangs of thugs went from flat to flat, helping themselves to anything that took their fancy.

Not all crimes were that violent then. Some criminals took to poking poles with hooks on them through people's windows to steal the valuables of the occupants within. They could even fish things out from under your bed. My flat had unexpectedly come off well during this period of chaos, which only ended when Idi Amin rounded up the *kondos*, as they were called, and, allegedly, threw them to the crocodiles in Lake Victoria.

It still amazes me how my two doors, both made of metal, resisted the bullets fired at their locks. I have not had the doors changed. I have grown fond of the dents the bullets made and have dined out on the story on more than one occasion.

It may have been that experience that sharpened my hearing. I have set myself a challenge. This is to define the sound that geckos make. I have a pencil and pad on a table at my bedside, as well as recording equipment. Jean has attached small microphones to the walls.

"It's a chirping sound," one of my notes says.

"No, it's a clicking."

Jean Bosco has been very good. He has tried various types of gecko in my room, taking them from their vivaria, having first rounded up the previous night's guests.

"It's chuk-chuk, chuk," I wrote down one night, having turned the sound up. "Like a boda-boda."

"No it's a churring. Nightjars."

The problem is that Jean is often in a hurry and I can lose track of the type of gecko on which I am conducting my experiment on any given night. There are technical problems too. My cave-like room has a terrible echo.

"Tut-tut-tut," one gecko calls out.

"Happy, happy, happeeee," cries another one that I had had delivered from Bali.

"Sounds like distant machine-gun fire," one note says.

"A car that won't start," says another.

"'Ow', like Eliza Doolittle's cry in George Bernard Shaw's play *Pygmalion*. Or did Eliza say, 'Ah-ah-ah-ow-ow-ow-oo!?'"

"No, it's like a sharp tapping on the window, followed by a raspberry."

"It's just 'Ah-er'."

"Like that raptor in Jurassic Park."

"No, it's geck-o, that's all."

That's where the word comes from! I had forgotten that *gekko* is a New Latin word, and that it comes from the old Indonesian-Malay word *gēkoq*, in imitation of the sound it makes.

"Ah, er, ah, er, ah, er," says a note here.

"Squeak. The chirp of a chick," says another.

I have been trying to resist the description that Mike Rainier, on a rare visit to my flat from his house on the edge of Maasai Mara in Kenya, once suggested: "In Vietnam we called them the 'F... you' insects, because of their sound."

Clive and Lilian called in to see me the other day.

"House Geckos say 'Tchik-tchak' which gives them the onamatopoeic Malay name Cikcak," Clive said, "'c' being pronounced 'ch' in Malay, and the terminal 'k' is a glottal stop."

Lilian said: "I think geckos make a noise like a 'chuck', in the ceilings, don't they? ... or a chitter too. You live in a friendly house if the geckos live with you."

I am coming to the conclusion that either I am going to be unable to pin the sound down or - and this is the real conclusion I am reaching - geckos have a much more complex communication system than we have hitherto realised.

I am also getting very frustrated with my equipment. It was old when Jean bought it and it keeps breaking down. The room itself has no curtains and no carpet. There is a strong echo effect. It feels as if I am living in an echo-chamber. Jean Bosco has begun to detect my frustration. I know he has.

"These geckos are doing our friend Gordon no good," he said to his wife.

He was, he said to her, sick and tired of picking up their

white-tipped droppings. They are everywhere, even on the bed-sheets and walls.

He came into my room late one night. He had had a few drinks. Bottles of wine had been left half-full at a reception at the embassy. I was feeling under the weather. I was half-asleep when he entered.

"I wish I could get rid of these blinking echoes, Jean Bosco," I muttered.

"Blinking gekkos"? he said, slurring his words.

"Yes, Jean."

"Do gekkos blink?" Jean Bosco muttered inaudibly.

While I was asleep, he put everything into a skip in the road above the flat, put out there for the rubbish that was being stripped away around Lugard's Fort. The fort is right next door. I used to reply to people, when asked where I lived, "Lugard's Fort". There was a rumour that a mosque dedicated to Colonel Gaddafi was going to be built up here.

I am not angry with Jean Bosco. It had all become too much for me. I know now that I am never going to be able to transcribe accurately the language of geckos.

Some of the creatures have made their way back into the flat. I am grateful for that. I just lie here now in the dark and listen to their tiny sounds. I am not an unhappy man.

My son writes to me now and then. He has landed a good job in Wall Street.

The Old Man and The Stride

I spotted him sitting on a bench. I have to say that he looked terrible. He had lost almost all of his hair, apart from some wispy grey bits at the side. In spite of being almost bald, he managed to have a very unkempt look about him. He looked as if he had literally been dragged through a hedge backwards. The lines on face resembled those deeply cut tribal markings that some Nuers have: wavy, horizontal ones on his forehead and vertical ruts like cart tracks down his cheeks. He clearly wasn't from Sudan. Nevertheless I felt that I should show respect to his advanced years, not that I was that young myself. I sat down next to him and engaged him courteously in conversation.

To break the ice, I asked him about the monument in front of us. It hadn't been there when I was last in Kampala, many years before. He explained that it is called "The Stride".

"Where are we exactly in Kampala?" I asked.

"We are behind the Parliament Gardens," he replied. The Serena Hotel is just there. He nodded in the direction of the hotel.

"Got you," I said.

"It was unveiled by the Queen of England."

"I didn't know that," I said.

He started coughing terribly. I didn't know what to do. I reached across and patted him on the back.

"It's all right, it's all right," he spluttered. "It'll go in a minute."

"Is it the pollution?" I asked looking towards the almost stationary traffic standing nose to tail on nearby Kintu Road. "I got a boda boda from the uni."

"No, it's not the car fumes," he replied. "It's the tobacco. I smoke four packs of cigarettes a day."

16

"Four packs a day!" I gasped.

"Yes, yes, eighty a day." He took out a packet of Sportsman. "The Government is discussing banning smoking in public. They are talking about a huge fine or jail for two months. I'll have to find somewhere else to sit."

The coughing started again.

"My goodness, you smoke like a chimney!" I said. I instantly regretted the comment.

He carried on coughing. I don't think he heard me. He heaved up a huge amount of sputum and spat it into a plastic carrier bag he had beside him.

"Can't stand people who spit on the ground," he wheezed. The storm abated. He began to recover a fairly normal breathing rhythm.

"So tell me about the statue," I said, changing the subject.

He looked up from the ground. I have never seen such bloodshot eyes! I put it down to the coughing fit he had just had but there was something more permanent-looking about their colour. I wondered if he had conjunctivitis or perhaps had suffered a burst blood vessel or even something worse. Was it drink, I wondered?

"The statue was put up to commemorate the Commonwealth Heads of Government Meeting in 2007." He spoke with a rasping, almost a rattling sound in the chest.

"CHOGM?" I asked.

"That's right."

He is an intelligent man, I thought. I popped the question.

"You know your stuff. Are you a graduate?"

"Yes, sir, I certainly am and proud of it. Best three years of my life."

"Bat Valley?

"Yes, Sir!" He said it in an ironical American way as if imitating a soldier addressing an officer. I wondered if he had been to America, or, perhaps had a career in the past in the Ugandan army.

I told him I had been a student there once and that I was in

Kampala on a brief visit for a conference at BVU. He listened with interest. I mentioned The New Life Club.

"Regular there. Not just there," he went on, "but nearly everywhere: Bubbbles O'Leary's, Iguana, Rider's Lounge, now shut, Just Kicking, Four Turkeys, The Bourbon Source of the Nile, Deuces, Zone 7, De Posh, Inferno Zar, the Abuja, The Junction, Yasigi's - I know them all," he said.

"You have certainly enjoyed your life," I commented.

"Yes, I certainly have," he said with satisfaction.

"You like a drink, then?" I asked.

He had another brief coughing fit, tapped his cigarette out on the ground, then lit a fresh one. I noticed that his fingers, as well as his mouth, were stained with nicotine.

"Yes, this is my poison," he said. He drew a bottle of waragi out of another bag. He took a huge swig, letting out a satisfied "Ah!"

"Want some?" he asked? I declined politely. I noticed, when he put the bottle to his lips, that his gums were bare. There wasn't a tooth in his head.

"Ah, well," I thought to myself. "It's the price you pay. He's obviously had a long, eventful and enjoyable life."

"The statue," he said, gaining a boost from the alcohol, "is the most expensive one ever put up in Uganda. It cost 150 million Uganda Shillings. He unscrewed the bottle top and had another gulp of his banana gin. The bottle said 'Uganda Waragi' on it. It is colourless like gin or vodka.

"Some expats called this drink 'war gin'. That's where the word comes from. The Baganda call it 'enguli'. That's the word in Luganda."

"War gin, waragi," I didn't know that.

"You see," he said with a smile. "It gave Buganda warriors Dutch courage."

"How much do you drink a day?" I felt I could ask that at that moment.

"Two, sometimes three bottles day. It depends."

"What!"

18

I was amazed. How could a man of his years drink so much? I had always believed that one had to slow down as one got older.

"Yes, two to three bottles." He screwed up his eyes to stare at the monument.

"It's made of aluminium," he said.

I thought I detected a silent burp.

"The man, the woman and the child symbolise the Commonwealth family of free nations moving forward together into the future."

I didn't want to interrupt while he was in full flow.

"It was created by Maria Naita, David Kigozi and Segamwenge Henry and others. There were eleven of them altogether."

"The Commonwealth as a nuclear family rather than as an extended family?" I asked

He started coughing again.

"It's not the cough that carries you off, it's the coffin they carry you off in," I ventured.

"That's ... a ... good one," he said. "No, no. That was not the sculptors' intention."

"Well, it looks like that."

"No, no, Dr George Kyeyune, who supervised the project, explained on TV that it depicts the emergence of a new family, the Commonwealth family. It's a metaphor, not a description of an actual African family."

"I see ... ." I must have sounded unconvinced.

"You yourself must have a huge extended family by now," I said."

"No, no, I am not married."

"Oh? Don't fancy it?"

"I don't need to. I have five girlfriends.

"Five!"

"Yes, five. I try to see at least two of them each day."

"Two a day!"

I didn't know whether to congratulate him or not. How could a man of his age have such stamina?

"I suppose they are getting on a bit", I said trying to suppress a pang of jealousy.

"No. All in their early twenties. Actually one is nineteen."

"What?"

"Yes."

I was beginning secretly to admire my new friend. He was an example to us all. All those cigarettes, all that waragi, all those mistresses, five mistresses. The fearlessness of it all!

A large bird with long spindly legs and a scrawny neck walked by.

"Marabou?" I asked. He nodded, not wanting to trigger another bout of coughing. He took another slug of waragi.

The stork had interrupted my train of thought. It looked so old.

"Looks ancient," I said.

"No, no, that's quite a young one," he said.

"The figures in that statue are traditionally dressed," I commented.

"Yes, but they are straining with their child to move into the future, to touch the future of the Commonwealth."

"You know, I think you are marvellous. Eighty cigarettes a day, two or three bottles of waragi, five girlfriends. It's amazing. I just don't know how a man of your age does it. Do you mind my asking how old you are exactly?"

"I am twenty-two." He got up to go.

"Where are you from?" It was a question I had been dying to ask him.

"Boston," he shouted.

"Boston Lincs or Boston Massachusetts?" He was out of earshot.

The Buffalo Men of Akagera

This isn't much of a story. I wasn't going to tell it at first but something in my head prompted me to include it.

Mike was from the States. He was part First Nation American, not that you would have known when you first met him. Growing up on a reservation, his mind was filled with ideas about the bison. He called it Tatanka. Early immigrants to America called it the buffalo.

Mike loved the whole range of creatures to which people over time have attached the label 'buffalo': the American Bison, technically speaking *Bison bison*; the European Bison, called *Bison bonasus*; the Indian 'Bison' (the Gaur or Seladang) *Bos gaurus* of South and South-East Asia. He held that the latter is very different from other buffaloes and bison. In China he studied the Water Buffalo or *Bubalus arnee*, now domesticated. In Africa it was the African or Cape Bufalo, *Syncerus caffer*, never domesticated, that filled his thoughts.

For him buffalo/bison symbolised abundance, generosity, courage, survival, hospitality, perseverance, wisdom interconnectivity, strength, honour, adaptability, sharing and many other qualities. The list went on and on. They stood for standing one's ground, gratitude, power, stability. The buffalo was, he said, a sacred creature in his culture and in many others.

Born in South Dakota, he was not pure Lakota but he spoke Lakota. He would come out with things like this, that when the white buffalo appeared in one's dream or in a daytime waking vision, it was a sign that one was about to achieve great prosperity.

He had come to Africa via China where he had done some lecturing, having first gained a good degree in Biology and

Philosophy from the University of South Dakota.

When Joe, a private tutor in Kampala, originally from Bedfordshire, met him, Mike had just come back from Burundi where he had been studying the place of the buffalo in a local religion. The first memory he had of the American was when Mike told him about a demi-god called Kiranga, the son of a king, who was killed by a buffalo during a hunt. The king's dead son had become a sort of intermediary between the human and the divine. If you needed help with something, a cure or a guarantee of a good crop, for example, you would address your prayers to him. Priests would, he said, become Kiranga during religious ceremonies. Women could also become Kiranga.

Joe had always been curious about bison and buffaloes. He had driven past them every day on Bison Hill on his way to work in St Albans. Now and then he would park his car halfway up the hill and go over to the wire fence that separated Whipsnade Zoo from the passing traffic. He would stand and stare at the creatures. They seemed out of place in the Chilterns.

One of Joe's prize possessions was an old post card of Buffalo Bill's buffaloes standing outside a pub in Luton attached to an old fashioned American cart.

In China, Mike told Joe, he had witnessed something really terrible. He had gone with some Chinese friends to a sort of arena. It was like a bullring. Two buffaloes had been released, each from either end of the ring. They had charged at each other at enormous speed, crashing head-on. They had died on the spot. Blood seeped into the mud from their broken skulls.

He told Joe that the Dong people of southern China enjoy buffalo fighting and that the Yi minority in south-western China fight bulls, both as part of a harvest festival called The Torch and to celebrate the Lunar New Year.

Understandably, given the reverence towards the animal that he had been taught when growing up in Dakota, the spectacle had thoroughly sickened Mike.

Together they went out in Mike's Land Rover to find buffaloes in East Africa's game parks. They were told by a park ranger in the Maasai Mara that a buffalo was sometimes called 'The Black Death' or 'The Widow Maker'. They are said to kill, the ranger told them, over two hundred people a year.

Mike and Joe would go to Kidepo Valley National Park in Uganda. It had once been Idi Amin's playground. Together they explored the dictator's derelict Katurum Lodge, abandoned when he was overthrown in 1979. Mike treasured a photograph he took of Joe standing under a sausage tree in front of the lodge.

They attended Kabaka Ronald Mutebi's coronation in 1993. By then they had become fixtures in Kampala's social scene. Mike had become a part-time lecturer in African Religion at Bat Valley and was in much demand for talks. Joe had landed some lucrative contracts tutoring the children of wealthy Ugandan families.

They had both received a formal invitation to the ceremony. As the new Kabaka was carried by, a friendly courtier whispered that the Buffalo Clan was responsible for the bark cloth on which the king sat when he was borne aloft at such times. No one, apart from a prince, could touch it. To do so would incur severe censure. The Buffalo Clan traditionally provided the Kabaka, he added, with one of his wives.

Joe and Mike drove down to Rwanda. They adored everything about the country, in spite of its bloody past. They would spend long weekends and holidays at a game lodge where they loved sampling the local fare. They found Rwanda enchanting.

They stopped the car at the side of a road near some trees in Akagera National Park.

"What's the matter with us?" Joe asked. "Why don't we just go and explore the forest over there?"

They locked the car and began to walk towards the trees with their binoculars, hoping to glimpse a distant buffalo.

They were three quarters of the way there, when a line of black buffaloes emerged from the trees. Joe remembered a scene in the film *The Battle of the Bulge* in which a line of

23

German Panzers came out suddenly from the Ardennes Forest.

They froze. The buffaloes froze. The two men turned and began to run. The buffaloes began to run. They were faster than Joe and Mike. Buffaloes can run at anything between thirty and forty miles an hour.

Joe was a good runner. Mike was not. Joe still played rugby now and then for Kampala. Neither was fast enough though. Usain Bolt has clocked twenty-eight miles an hour but Joe and Mike couldn't even do twenty.

They didn't make it to the car.

The Beautiful Butterfly People of Kanyawara

The university had been very gracious in agreeing to host the conference at its field station in Kanyawara. I had managed to get hold of some funds from Brussels for the event.

It was a difficult moment. The British had just voted to leave the European Union. Brexit had set passions running high. If you were for leaving the EU, you were a racist. If you voted remain, you were a traitor. The country had not been so divided for years.

The conference title was 'The Butterfly'. It was held under the auspices of the Departments of Literature and Biology at Bat Valley. The Dean of the Faculty of Humanities was chairing the proceedings.

I started the event off by reading a poem I had written some years earlier. Foolishly, I had allowed myself to be persuaded to publish it in prose in one of my books on Africa, changing it dramatically, removing its poetic character. The colleagues who did that were immersed in the old ways of thinking about writing poetry, the one they had learned at school. Poems for them had to rhyme. I had always felt that this could create an absurd effect. I pointed out that rhyme began as a form of mnemonics that was used by poets in the Middle Ages to remember their lines, a system for assisting the memory as they recited their long epic poems at court. I called poets who are addicted to the use of excessive rhyme, 'the jingle jangle brigade'. A friend who overheard me say that thought I was being racist and was referring to an ethnic minority in my home town. I managed to disabuse him. We call him 'London's witch-hunter in chief'.

Anyway, here is my poem. It's called 'Butterflies'. It begins with an epigram by Rabindranath Tagore.

"The butterfly counts not months but moments and has time enough."

This quotation was met with thunderous applause from the conference attendees. I went on.

Butterflies

I used to ride in Africa
through clouds of butterflies.

Black, yellow and red,
green and white,
they would sting my eyes.

They would stick to the sunscreen
on my face, on my mouth and cheeks,
bright like the paint of a brave.

As straight as a die
ran the road that crossed
Mabira Forest.

They want to cut down
the old arching trees
of the forest in Mukono
and in its place
grow sugar cane.

Just like the fruit bats
on Kampala Road,
our butterflies survive
on borrowed time.

My reading was met with polite applause. I had worked on it the previous night and had not been entirely satisfied with the result. It kept changing shape. Be that as it may, I felt that the conference had got off to reasonable start. At least I had established my Green credentials.

There were several good papers. There was one in particular, 'Shakespeare and Butterflies'. Over the years I had discovered that educated Ugandans knew Shakespeare much better than I did. I had heard on good authority that Prime Minister, later President, Obote, would, back in the sixties, bamboozle or simply put down his colleagues in cabinet meetings with quotes from the Bard's plays. I managed to get hold of a copy of Claire Semwanga's paper and ringed this quote.

KING LEAR
No, no, no, no! Come, let's away to prison:
We two alone will sing like birds i' the cage:
When thou dost ask me blessing, I'll kneel down,
And ask of thee forgiveness: so we'll live,
And pray, and sing, and tell old tales, and laugh
At gilded butterflies, and hear poor rogues
Talk of court news; and we'll talk with them too,
Who loses and who wins; who's in, who's out;
And take upon's the mystery of things,
As if we were God's spies: and we'll wear out,
In a wall'd prison, packs and sects of great ones,
That ebb and flow by the moon.

Claire explained: "To gild a butterfly, to coat it in gold,

would be to destroy it. It would not be able to fly. It is not possible to wrap something fragile up to make it look more beautiful." Many in the conference were hanging on her words.

At this point another beautiful young Ugandan post-graduate student stood up and delivered a wonderful paper on the word butterfly. She pointed out that in Middle English it was called, amongst other things, a 'buterflie', whilst in Old English, over a thousand years ago, it was 'butterfleoge'.

She linked it to Old Dutch words. The English, she explained, were a sort of tribe that formed on what is now the Dutch coast before setting off for England.

"The Old Dutch word is 'botervlieg'," she said, adding that there was another word, 'boterschijte'.

"Butter Scheiße, Butter shite!" exclaimed our German colleague from Leipzig, apparently unable to control himself. "That is very ugly!" The recent Brexit vote had put him on edge.

The young student, Dembe Binaisa, explained patiently that people in those days may have thought that butterflies' excrement resembled butter. She surmised that 'butter-shit' was replaced fairly soon by 'butter-fly', for obvious reasons. She added that possibly people back then associated butterflies with witches and that witches in butter-fly form, shape-shifters, stole butter and milk.

"Yes, yes, I know all about that," Hans muttered disagreeably.

"In Norway we say 'summerfugl'," Bjorn, a participant from that country volunteered,

"Very nice, said Dembe." All the men's eyes were on her. She had them in the palm of her hand.

"In Yiddish we say 'zomerfeygele'," a colleague from East London University called out, trying to be noticed.

"In Zaire it is 'bulubulu'," cried out a gentleman from the University of Lubumbashi. "At least, that's what is in Tshiluba."

"Beautiful," sighed Dembe. 'In Luganda it is 'ekiwojjolo'. Do you know the song 'Kiwojjolo'?"

"Sing it, Dembe, sing it!" the dean said.

Dembe burst into song. The audience gave her a standing ovation.

The dean, Dr Bakabulindi, not wishing the conference to become too ... Afrocentric, leant towards the group representing the European Union. He was very aware that Brussels was about award cultural grants to Central and East African universities.

"And in Europe?" he said smiling courteously.

"Le papillon," Henri, the French academic, Henri Legrand responded. He continued in French: "It is the most delicate of words for the most delicate of creatures. You can feel the eloquence of the French language in that word, pa-pi-llon." Participants from Rwanda, Burundi, Zaire and the Central African Republic clapped enthusiastically.

"And in Spain?" the dean asked.

"It's 'mariposa'," replied Juan Manuel from Deusto, San Sebastian campus. Can't you just feel the gentle opening and closing of wings in that word. Ma-ri-PO-sa. Can't you just see the colours?"

There was polite applause. The audience didn't get the second point.

"We have already had the pleasure of hearing Miss Binaisa talk about the word in English. Dr Ironside, would you like to add anything?" the dean asked.

"Butterfly, butterfly, the word imitates the graceful movement of the insect. Butterflies flutter by, flutter by."

I made a fluttering movement with my hand. Dembe told me later in Paddy's Bar that I had had a mad glint in my eyes as I did that.

"Yes, er, yes," the dean said respectfully.

He knew that the next person was the key to the university getting a grant. He turned his whole body round to face our Leipzig colleague.

"Dr Bachhuber?"

"It's 'schmetterling'," Hans Bachhuber called out rather loudly. I felt that he was seething with repressed resentment about something but I couldn't work out what. Mind you, I often felt that about him.

You could hear a pin drop. Nobody clapped. Many in the audience were still thinking of the way he had scornfully dismissed Dembe's reference to the Old Dutch word 'boterschijte'.

"It's from 'schmetten', meaning 'cream', referring to the way witches used to change into butterfies to steal the cream. Or so people believed, In Low German is it is 'botterlicker', butter-licker."

He looked around the auditorium. He felt he was beginning to lose his composure. His impeccable English accent began to break down as he surveyed the rows of expressionless faces.

"And what is wrong with 'SCHMETTERLING'?" he cried out.

Realising that he had committed a faux pas, Hans tried to lighten the atmosphere by telling a joke.

"I was driving my car in Busoga. A Ugandan policeman pulled me over to the side of the road. He said, 'Sir, do you realise that there are two poisonous snakes on your windscreen?'

Of course, I replied. They are my vinscreen vipers."

Silence.

"You know, wiper - viper. We have difficulty with the English 'w'."

"Thank you, Dr Bachhuber, said the dean. I think we'll adjourn for lunch at that point."

"Let's go for a lager, Hans," I whispered in his ear.

The Chameleon of Buntuntumula

B ob had studied Education at Bat Valley University but had rebelled against what was taught there. He swore, when he left Bat Valley, that he would devote his life to developing a correct theory of education for a developing nation.

He went to live in a remote village in Buganda, Buntuntumula, north of Luwero, where he set up a private boarding school, Saint Francis's Preparatory College. There was no control or inspection of what he did. He had a totally free hand. The school had attracted an enormous grant from an American philanthropist. Money was no object and, in addition, the fees were substantial. Bob was planning on moving the school to Kampala.

Needless to say, his school became very popular with the expanding East African middle classes. He was getting children into some of the best schools: King's College Budo, Gayasa High School, Namilyango College, Uganda Martyrs' Secondary, Mount Saint Mary's College Namagunga, Mengo Senior School. In Kenya some went to the Aga Khan Academy or the Rift Valley Academy, in Tanzania, to Feza Boys and Feza Girls. One even went to Eton. Some parents in England had started sending their offspring to Saint Francis.

Bob stumbled on his master plan one night when he had had too much to drink and woke up face to face with a chameleon. *"Don't roll your blood-shot eyes at me / I can see that you've been on a spree"*, he muttered, quoting lines from a song that often came back to him. Suddenly his attitude changed. He stopped scolding the creature. It was as if a light

31

had come on his head. He knew what he had to do. His syllabus would be based on a special type of programme.

A whole term's work concentrates on the chameleon. Other terms involve lizards, snakes, bats, geckos, crocodiles, etc. Children are placed in houses bearing the names of some of these creatures. Bob's idea is that pupils should learn to be in maximum harmony with their surroundings. Rather than despising their country, they should become proud of it. His ideas are considered revolutionary. Experts come from around the world to see how he achieves his good results.

English classes are devoted to describing children's pet chameleons. One star pupil, from Meru in Tanzania, produced a Jackson chameleon. She compared it to a triceratops. She noticed that her chameleon, a male, had three horns, one on the nose, and one over the ridge above each eye.

Bob encouraged her to explore the dinosaur theme. Children started asking all sorts of questions. Why were there no dinosaurs in Africa? They discovered that there had been but that researchers had been simply too lazy to venture forth in difficult terrain to look for them. Lucy comes out with rare phrases like "rostral horn" - the one on the nose - and "preocular horns", those over the eyes. Bob is proud of his pupils' command of long words.

All learning is in English. Bob insists on BBC English. Revolutionary in most aspects, he is conservative in that respect. He discourages the use of "Uglish" - pronounced "You-glish" in Uganda. Words like "benching", referring to the act of dropping in on somebody in whom you have a romantic interest, and "wolokosso", meaning loose talk, and "vacist", a student on holiday, are strictly off-limits. As things stand at the moment, this has had the opposite effect. The ban has stimulated their use.

African stories are not neglected in the syllabus. Popular ones include: 'Anansi and the Chameleon', 'The Curse of the Chameleon' (from KwaZulu-Natal) and 'Ananse's Funeral'. Walter Bgoya's 'The Chameleon Who Could Not Change Her

Colour' is often borrowed from the school library. The brightest pupils are introduced to Chekhov's tale 'A Chameleon'.

Arithmetic is slanted towards the theme of the term: "There are ten chameleons and fifty insects. Each chameleon captures five insects with his long tongue. How many insects are left?" "There are twenty chameleons. Each one lays ten eggs. How many eggs are laid in total?" The children love it.

Geography classes involve colouring in maps of the world with the places where chameleons live: the Veiled Chameleon of Arabia, the Panther Chameleon of Madagascar, Jackson's Chameleon of Kenya and northern Tanzania (and Hawaii and Florida). They colour in Spain, Portugal and the parts of Asia where chameleons are found.

English classes can be pitched at a high level because of the school's daring approach. Bob is now rigorously selecting his intake. The children love detecting and analysing references to chameleons and other creatures in Shakespeare, for example:

"The chameleon's dish: I eat the air, promise-crammed; you cannot feed capons so."

"Who wrote that?" he will ask. A forest of hands will go up.

"William Shakespeare (born 26 April 1564, died 23 April 1616. *Hamlet*, Act II, Scene 1.)", comes the reply.

Bob allows a certain amount of rote learning, provided it reinforces the school's objectives. "A happy man or woman is one who is in harmony with his or her environment," he often repeats.

"I can add colours to the chameleon,
Change shapes with Proteus for advantages,
And set the murderous Machiavel to school.
Can I do this, and cannot get a crown?
Tut, were it farther off, I'll pluck it down."

Who said that?" Bob asks.

"Gloucester in *Henry VI*," comes the reply from the class. This party trick is often performed by Year Six children (age ten to eleven) before visiting philanthropists and benefactors.

He tells the children that people once believed that chameleons could live on air and that Shakespeare compared the creature to love: "*The chameleon Love can feed on the air.*"

"*Two Gentlemen of Verona*", the children will chant.

It isn't just snippets of Shakespeare they are introduced to. Jonathan Swift is part of their stock of quotes:

"*The chameleon, who is said to feed upon nothing but air, has of all the animals the nimblest tongue.*"

"*Thoughts on Various Subjects*, 1714," the children call out.

Swift's words are included in the text book that Bob has written for the school. Sales of the book on Amazon are going through the roof.

Alumni from his school have become pillars of strength in East African society. Bob spends hours debunking the theory that chameleons were sinister and unlucky creatures, reptiles to be feared. A subsidiary aim of his is to free his charges' minds of superstition. He fears that Africa is in danger of being swamped again by superstition and that his task is to fight it and to reverse the trend.

Religious Studies classes include an examination of African creation myths. One particular story, widespread in Africa, is that the chameleon was responsible for human mortality. According to Kenya's Kamba people, Bob tells his pupils, when Ngai Mulungu, the all-powerful God, created the world, it was his intention that humans should live forever. Mulungu sent the chameleon to deliver his news to man; but, in true chameleon fashion, the reptile, as is his nature, dillied and dallied. To add to Humanity's woes, the chameleon stammered while delivering his divine news and the message was lost forever.

He told the pupils that the myth takes different paths throughout Africa. As in the Kenyan version, in Malawi, Mozambique and Tanzania it is said that God had given the message to the chameleon but was overheard by the lizard, who, being swifter, ran ahead to pass on the news. The lizard misheard the Lord's words and informed the people that they

34

were destined to die and there would be no eternal life for them. When the chameleon finally arrived with the real story, he was ridiculed by the people who told him that he was wrong and that they already knew that they would die and that death would be the end of everything. From that moment on the poor chameleon was branded a liar, a cheat and a creature never to be trusted.

Bob's efforts turned his pupils' view of the chameleon upside down. To this day the belief lingers across Africa that Humanity's eventual destiny has been the result of the actions of the slow-moving and hesitant chameleon, resulting in the animal being greatly feared and hated. Old Franciscans proudly step in whenever they hear this said and correct the story.

He explains that in early Christianity, the chameleon was used to symbolize Satan who, like the chameleon, could change his appearance to deceive humankind but that now Christians do not believe that. This has helped the children to change their view of the creature. It also helped them in some way to attune to modern Christianity. Bob's sponsors are happy with his work.

Bob is a Christian. He allows visiting missionaries to spread the message that the chameleon is good because he or she, the chameleon, is charged by God to convey the message that Humanity is immortal. He encourages them to equate the chameleon with Jesus Christ, the herald of eternal life. Pictures adorn the school's walls combining images of chameleons with Christ on the Cross.

Art classes are devoted to chameleons for a whole term. The children are encouraged to draw the creatures: their feet resembling those of parrots, their prehensile tails, their scales, their eyes and their tongues as long as their bodies.

In her Art class Lucy strives to mix the right colours to describe 'Tricksy', her triceratops-like chameleon. She creates mainly bright greens and some yellows and blues as well. She tells her class if her pet is off-colour. It changes colour, she explains, according to his mood and health. The temperature can also trigger changes, she adds.

Depending on the year's budget, the school even goes to the lengths of inviting artists to the school. This was the Acholi Art teacher Saul's idea. He is a Bat Valley graduate. Painters from around the world are willing to come and show their work to the children.

Visiting artists will even do paintings in class. Gwenn Semeel gave a talk on her paintings, including the one of a panther chameleon *Up On The Catwalk*. The children are totally blown away by her images. Eli Wolfe's *Chillin Chameleon Painting* is in the syllabus, as are *Chameleon with Orchids* by Genevieve Esson. Wajanja's *Colourful Chameleon* is very popular as is *Green Chameleon* by Lanjee Chee.

History lessons include references to views of African animals over the centuries. They are taught that the word 'chameleon' comes from the Greek words for 'On the ground', '*khamal*', and lion, *león*, and that the philosopher Aristotle, wrote the words, "more changeable than a chameleon" three hundred and forty years before the birth of Christ. They are told that the word chameleon, after that, soon meant a fickle person, one who can change to fit in with anybody according to circumstances. They are told, incidentally that Idi Amin was sometimes like that.

So that things do not become too po-faced and serious, and possibly as a way of arming school leavers to cope with future taunts, year six are allowed to make jokes about the chameleon. This caused a problem recently.

A donor arrived from America. "I have a joke, sir," Musoke called out. "A chameleon walks into a bar...

... but nobody saw him."

"Hum!" said Bob, rolling his eyes. The children laughed. A smile lingered on the visiting benefactor's ruddy face.

"What do you call an incredibly rich chameleon, sir?" Judith Nalongo asked, raising her hand.

"Go on," said Bob.

"A multi-chameleonaire!"

The class laughed. The Good Samaritan beamed.

Betty Bakabulindi piped up.

"A chameleon went to the job centre in Kampala. He said, 'Oh yes, I am a good team player. I know how to blend in.'"

The benefactor smiled.

"Time to finish now," Bob said.

"Just one more, Mr Tingrith," Angel Nabulungi cried.

"All right, then, Angel. Just one more."

It had been organised as a prank. Angel's burning ambition was to become a pop singer.

"Boy George, Class, Culture Club. One, two three, KARMA CHAMELEON!" she shouted.

The class went wild and started singing and dancing:

Karma Karma Karma Karma Karma Chameleon
You come and go, you come and go.
Loving would be easy
if your colours were like my dream
Red, gold and green,
red, gold and green.

Bob was delighted. "Fearless spontaneity," he wrote in his diary. With the palm of his hand he banged the top of the desk at which he was sitting in time to the song, allowing his head and shoulders to dip and rise in harmony.

He swung round to look at Quinton, the wealthy visitor from Salt Lake City. He had forgotten he was there. Quinton was heading for the door. His face had gone from a bright flamingo pink to a deathly, pallid white. He was not amused.

The Chicken Man of Mbarara

There was anger then, in Africa.
Horace, my African-American friend, was from the wrong side of the tracks in Detroit. I was not sure why he had come to Africa. He was doing some research on chickens at Bat Valley University but I felt that, deep down, he was looking for something else.

He had married a Mugandan and they had two children. Horace was always rather off-hand with me. Sometimes he seemed angry with me. The truth is I had no real idea where he was coming from. In 1960s England we didn't understand what was happening in America.

It was 1966. We were at the top of the hill, near the Kabaka's Palace, when it happened. Three soldiers stepped out, holding rifles. Their faces and their bodies were thin. They were from the north of Uganda. My light green Ford Zephyr 4 screeched to a stop.

"Kwenda chini", one shouted, pointing his gun.

What did he mean? All three of them were shaking with fear.

"Horace," I whispered, "Does he mean 'Get out of the car', 'Get on to the ground' or 'Go back down the hill?'"

A shot rang out. A bullet broke the glass of the small, triangular ventilation window by my right hand and embedded itself in the door at my side, just a few inches away.

Horace was already out, lying on the ground. I stepped out.

'Lie down', Horace hissed.

'Get up!' I hissed back. "You are presenting yourself as a victim."

An Englishwoman started screaming frantically for help in the bushes. I think she was English but she could have been Ugandan. She had a cultured voice. There was nothing we could do.

"Get up off the ground, Horace", I shouted.

It was then that they started kicking him. Horace started to laugh as the boots struck his back and stomach.

"Why are you laughing?" I gasped between my teeth.

"I get the **** kicked out of me in America and I get it kicked out of me here, in the land of my fathers", he gasped, as the boots thudded into his ribs.

Horace moved his family to Tanzania. We had a farewell do for him. He felt even more distant. I swear I could detect a flicker of anger in his eyes as we said goodbye.

We met up again, some years later, in 'Jackie's Bar' in Haile Selassie Avenue in Dar es Salaam. It is popular today with Africans, Americans, Australians and the Chinese. We were tucking into chips *mayai* and beef *mishkaki* when he told me that some Tanzanians didn't know what to make of him. Was he a missionary? Was he a teacher? Was he an aid worker? What was he? He said that he just wanted to hang out for a bit in 'the land of his fathers'.

He told me that he liked keeping chickens and that he kept them healthy by giving them frequent injections. They all survived the Newcastle's Disease outbreak that decimated the flocks of his neighbours. The villagers couldn't understand it. Rumours began to spread.

One day they stopped his Land Rover. Someone shouted out, "He's carrying *mumias*" (local vampires). The angry crowd pulled him out and set fire to his vehicle. A passing policeman stopped him being strung up on the spot.

"He's a witch!" someone cried.

At this, he was arrested, but was later released by the local police inspector who decided that a man from Detroit would, on balance, probably not be into black magic.

Horace moved back to Uganda to try to make another fresh start. He opened a chicken farm near Mbarara.

Funny things could happen in Uganda at that time. One day, in a shop, in either 1972 or 1973, Horace inadvertently handed over a note from which someone had removed the dictator Idi Amin's eyes, leaving just holes. He was immediately expelled from the country, leaving his wife and children to get out as best they could.

I had an email from him the other day. I don't know, there still seems to be some anger in him.

The Crane Lady of Mperwerwe

Jane hailed from Hertfordshire. Whenever she glimpsed colourful male pheasants standing amongst the new shoots of corn at the side of the St Albans to Hemel Hempstead road, her spirits soared.

It was not until she went to Uganda that she fell in love with the grey crested crane, Uganda's national symbol. Her enthusiasm for the crane led her to develop signs of eccentric behaviour. Some say she got carried away. Secretly she had decided to plough a narrow furrow. If she could become the world authority on the crested crane, she might be able to establish a new academic area: Bio-Anthropology - the study of similarities between human and animal behaviour.

She homed in almost immediately on one of the most interesting aspects of crane behaviour: their dancing. She spent months wading through wetlands, swamps and the edges of lakes filming the birds' spectacular courtship dance.

She joined the Bat Valley Cultural Society, co-sponsored by the Anthropology and Biology departments. Members of the society clapped politely as she mimicked the crane's dance, strapping feathers and even wings to her arms.

She gained the nickname among staff of Kampala's Isadora Duncan, although to most she was 'plain Jane Crane'. She had even performed the crane dance, craning her neck and so on, on the stage of the National Theatre. The jury was out on the performance. Some were troubled by it, others were full of admiration. The act improved when a male ballet dancer joined her. Some critics described their act in glowing terms. Twice a year they performed 'The Crested Crane Courtship' dance in the Crested Crane Hotel in Jinja. The manager paid them well.

Jane was fascinated by the crane's apparent loyalty and

41

devotion to one partner. She had a row of books in her office at Bat Valley on sexually monogamous birds. The definition of monogamy she adopted was the strictest one possible. She particularly admired zebra finches, geese, eagles and swans.

She pored over references to cranes as symbols of fidelity in other cultures, for example the red-crowned crane in China and Japan. She had a framed collection of 1000 yen notes that used cranes as a design, as well as examples from Ugandan coins and notes depicting the bird. Above her desk was the black, red and yellow Uganda national flag with the image of the crested crane at its centre.

She energetically encouraged students to undertake post-graduate study on the aspects of crested crane behaviour that intrigued her. Pair bonding for life was her area but she had graduates working on the body language of the crane. They had identified more than ninety different types of visual display used by cranes to preserve social order. Other students were working on similar displays among humans, salutes, curtsying, funny secret society handshakes, etc. The eventual aim was to compare the two, the crane and the human. A difficulty had arisen. Humans use words to keep order, e.g. the English and their irony.

Another student, Boniface Mpepwe, was investigating 'The Crested Crane and Vocalisation' and was finding some similarities with humans' vocal messages.

Calvin Heine from Pittsburg was looking into the question of socialisation. He had to be careful not to tread on Jane's toes as this involved the study of bonded pairs as well as families within a larger group. He side-stepped that difficulty by focusing more on the way pairs protect their young, similar to humans.

Claire Belfast from Trinidad was comparing the lifespans of humans and cranes. Her thesis included a study of Asian myths of the bird's longevity. Some cultures have stories of cranes living a thousand years, she noted. She established that the bird lives roughly thirty to forty years and that this was the average lifespan of a human being before the Industrial Revolution and the advent of modern medicine.

Dawn Hudson from Ghana was working on the body dimensions of the crane, together with its locomotion. She found that their height varies from one hundred to two hundred centimetres, confirming her working hypothesis that they are the same height as humans. She was researching ancient Greek myths that cranes and pygmies used to engage in battles at the headwaters of the Nile. This involved trips to museums in Europe to examine depictions of battles between humans and cranes on Greek pottery. She had visited the Hermitage Museum in St Petersburg to view 'Pygmy Fighting Crane', the Athenian red-figure vase of the fifth century BC.

Horace Dalyrimple from Wadham College Oxford was establishing links with the Art Department and together they were creating and curating exhibitions of crested crane paintings in the Bat Valley University Library. They were planning to approach galleries in Kampala: Sestreet, AKA, Karibu, Magina, Umpja, Afriart and others with a view to putting on a major crested crane event, with sculptures in bronze and wood, decorated plates and metal screens depicting the bird. The Uganda Tourism Board had been approached for finance.

It was 'all systems go' in Jane's area. She was a rising star. There seemed to be no stopping her. Her fame had spread beyond Uganda. *The Independent* in London was planning a feature on her. Her enthusiasm for her subject grew and it was infectious. She had fallen in love with her subject and others did too.

She even kept a crested crane as a pet. She had rescued the bird as a chick. Its parents had died at the hands of hunters. The crane had become an endangered species owing to human encroachment on its wetland habitat. Fields were being created in their place. She had designed a costume to prevent the chick from imprinting on a human. It didn't work. They became inseparable. It was rumoured that Jane could be seen driving around with 'Cranky', as she called him, beside her in her open-topped Mini Cooper Convertible. She became a topic of intense gossip in the Bat Valley staff bar. Rumours spread that the bird was sleeping in a basket in her bedroom. The bird had grown into a handsome male.

I was standing at the university staff bar. I saw a familiar face. It was Edgar from Development Economics.

"Have your heard the latest?" he sniggered.

Members of other departments were becoming envious of Jane's success. Things like that happen in academia. Some smelled favouritism on the part of the vice-chancellor. Jane was the flavour of the month. Edgar was clearly one of her enemies. He could barely contain himself.

"Jane was seen in Mperwerwe Cinema Hall the other day."

He spluttered with mirth, spraying beer over the counter. Stories about Jane and her companion in that particular cinema had been circulating for some time.

"A man behind her saw what appeared to be a crested crane sitting next to her."

He was banging his fist on the bar now, trying to control himself.

"Anyway, this chap reached forward, patted the crane on the shoulder and asked, 'Are you a crested crane?'

'Yes,' came the answer.

'What are you doing watching this film?' this friend of mine asked."

I thought that any minute the economist was going to wet himself.

"Go on," I said, keen to see how the bad joke would pan out.

"The crane turned round and answered, 'Well, I liked the book!'"

The Crocodilophile of Mukusu Island

Gustave was a strange character. He was a crocodilophile. Gustave wasn't his real name. He named himself after a gigantic crocodile that inhabited the waters of Lake Tanganyika.

Most people shy away from crocodiles. Not Gustave. He loved them. He was, in fact, obsessed with them. Nobody is quite sure how this happened. Some argued that he was separated from his mother at an early age when he was packed off to a private boarding school. Others say that it is the result of his incredible wealth. Gustave does not have to work. His father, who made a fortune in something to do with mobile phones and banking, had died young, leaving his fortune to his son. Whatever it was, Gustave had great difficulty in forming relationships. He was unable to attract a permanent girlfriend.

He was aware of his family history. An old uncle had whispered in his ear once that he belonged to the crocodile clan. That was the moment when the seed of Gustave's interest in crocodiles was planted.

Like many people who come into money, Gustave started to travel. His incredible wealth – he was a multi-multi-millionaire – enabled him to buy wonderful *objets d'art*.

The idea that he belonged to a special crocodile clan began to take root in his mind. It was the Nile crocodile that filled his thoughts. He decided to comb the Nile Valley from top to bottom, starting in Egypt and working his way down, seeking out references to the crocodile.

What was it about the crocodile that had so intrigued the ancient Egyptians, he asked himself? He visited a temple in

Egypt that had been dedicated to the crocodile. What had lain behind this crocodile cult? He couldn't crack the mystery, until one day, sitting by the Nile, he got talking to an Egyptian fisherman who had good local knowledge.

"Ah, those crocodiles are clever," Saleh, the Arab fisherman said, "yes, damn clever. They know just how high the river is going to rise and they lay eggs in the sand just above what will be the high water mark in any given year."

This comment was like a flash of lightning in Gustave's mind. Of course, a priesthood that could predict the level of the river, whether or not it was going to flood, would have had enormous power. No wonder they revered the crocodile! Such priests would have near-total control over their followers. They could tell them where to plant their seed. In other words, they could teach them how to survive.

Gustave began to amass a collection of crocodile-related jewellery. It filled the place he had built on his Crocodile Island in the Sseses. There was even a room dedicated to crocodile mummies. Gustave had managed to get hold of several of these in the wake of the war in Iraq that had caused such chaos in the Cairo antiques market.

He combed Africa for art that reflected his interest, masks and statues, etc. He spent a great deal of money in Mombasa having doors carved by Swahili craftsmen with the crocodile motif.

He collected Gambian coins, the ones with crocodiles stamped on them. He visited several times the sacred crocodile pool in The Gambia called Kachikaly that serves as a prayer-ground for visitors.

He had beautiful Dogon crocodile totems fashioned out of clay on his patio walls. He felt protected by them. He had been captivated by their beauty in a visit to Amani village in Mali. He was struck by the fact that the villagers kept a pool full of crocodiles in the village that do not harm anybody.

His retreat on Mukusu Island contained huge glass tanks for his collection of crocodiles. Lit like aquaria they formed one side of the area where his superb swimming pool had been constructed, just a stone's throw from a luxury hotel.

Gustave's interest in crocodiles took an unusual turn. He felt an overwhelming desire to save them. He began to buy up fields around his mansion in which he created pools. With his helicopter he would fly to the rescue of any crocodile that had got into difficulties.

When he learned that ruthless men and women were developing huge crocodile farms in Africa to feed a growing fashion for crocodile meat, he saw red. He began a Facebook campaign denouncing the vile trade. A dedicated website teemed with photographs of the disgusting, filthy water in which the creatures were reared.

He financed a protest group devoted to disrupting the trade. Questions were being raised about "crocodile terrorism" in parliament in Kenya. The emergency caused by jihadists put that concern onto the back burner.

Within Uganda he began to finance protests outside crocodile leather factories. His Facebook page contained denunciations of celebrities who insisted on being seen in public clutching crocodile leather handbags. The Minister for Tourism began to monitor his activities.

"Crocs not crocodiles" screeched one headline on his personal page. He attempted to launch in Uganda the hideous croc shoes fashion that was sweeping London. He bought up stocks of used car tyres and employed a small army of men and women to cut them into the shape of clogs.

The tide began to turn. Patience was beginning to run out. Gustave had nobody close who could warn him. He became a very lonely man, devoting more and more hours to virtue-signalling on the internet. "Hunting Crocodiles Is wrong", "Crocodile Meat Is Bad For You", "Ban The Vile Trade in Crocodile Skin", "Shed a Tear for the Crocodile" are just some of the campaign headlines that screamed at you from his page.

He invited people from all over the world to sign petitions that he would deliver in person to the President. People in high places decided that enough was enough. Something had to be done.

Gustave's increasing loneliness and isolation intensified his eccentricity. He desperately wanted to find a partner but he was becoming psychologically incapable of knowing how to go about it. Meanwhile, the vultures were circling. A plan had been formed to render him harmless.

As was mentioned above, Gustave had a large swimming pool. Its lights could be seen from the windows of the nearby hotel. It was very tempting for young tourists who had been told that swimming in the lake was out of bounds, owing to the risk of contracting bilharzia. The pool was a beautiful sight. It had picnic tables under palm trees. It was dotted with avocado and paw-paw trees laden with fruit.

One evening, Gustave went out to his pool to pick some avocadoes. As he approached the pool, armed with a bucket, he heard shouts of glee. He drew closer and saw a group of young Scandinavian women skinny-dipping in his pool. Deep down he knew that this was bound to happen. Deep down, he knew that he had planned it.

He coughed to draw attention to himself. The girls looked up at him and saw an obese, heavily perspiring, middle-aged man. They swam towards the deep end.

"We are not coming out until you go back into the house," one of them shouted.

Gustave pressed the button on a remote in his pocket. Curtains automatically opened to reveal his huge crocodile aquarium. Rows of grinning teeth pressed up against the glass.

"I didn't come out to watch you beautiful young ladies swim or to make you get out of the water naked. I came to feed the crocodile." He held up the bucket.

The following day, police arrived by launch. Gustave was seen getting into it in handcuffs. No more was heard of him in Uganda.

Rumour has it that he now lives in Dar es Salaam where he has formed a strange religious order.

The Herpetologist of Nabajuzzi Swamp

Mukasa is a lecturer in Biology at Bat Valley University in Kampala. He is especially interested in frogs. In fact, he lives for frogs.

He bought land and property at the edge of the Nabajjuzi Swamp. Nabajjuzi lies near the main road between Kampala and Western Uganda. Tourists on their way to see elephants, gorillas and chimpanzees call in to marvel at the collection he has formed in his indoor research centre and in the small lagoons and ponds he has created.

Frogs are his way of seeing the world. He travels all over Africa and beyond looking for them. He makes frequents trips to The Democratic Republic of the Congo, Burundi and Sudan.

He is very fond of African Dwarf Frogs, also called Dwarf Clawed Frogs. His search for them has taken him to the Congo River Basin, Nigeria and Cameroon and to many other forested parts. They have become his pets. He loves observing them in their tanks, as they use their webbed feet to stuff food down their throats. He is fascinated by the hyobranchial pump they have to draw and suck food into their mouths. He is ecstatic when he sees them use the claws on their feet to tear pieces from anything living, dying or dead.

Another of his favourites is the Goliath Frog. His pride and joy is one that weighs seven pounds. He watches them develop from tadpoles that start the normal size but become huge. He loves the way they whistle when they are engaged in courtship rituals. He tells his friends that he acquired "the biggest frog in the world" during an expensive trip to a river in a forest in Equatorial Guinea.

His is very proud of his Madagascan Tomato Frog that he found in the island's Antongil Bay. At times he feels he could eat the red and plump tomato-like creature, as big as a beefsteak tomato, such is his love for his pet.

He even has a Latin American section in his reptile house. He had it built to house Blue Poison Dart Frogs, Mimic Poison Frogs, Golden Poison Frogs and Red-Eyed Tree Frogs, also called Monkey Frogs, because of their ability to leap a good distance. He loves scaring visitors, telling them that a fraction of the Golden Poison Frog's venom can kill a human. Within seconds he can tell if a person has a trace of ranidaphobia, a fear of frogs, in him or her and he will home in on them with hair-raising stories.

The South African section of the above building contains Sand Toads, Amatola Toads, Leopard Toads, Olive Toads, Northern Pygmy Toads, Bush Squeakers, Mottled Shovel-Nosed Frogs, Natal Ghost Frogs, Table Mountain Ghost Frogs, Marbled Rubber Frogs, Hogsback Frogs, Snoring Puddle Frogs, Knocking Sand Frogs and many more. He loves to regale visitors with the myths and legends associated with frogs, such as those about frog spirits.

His colleagues at Bat Valley are worried about Mukasa. The years are going by and he shows no sign of settling down. Rumours have begun to circulate, none of which is true. Uganda has been going through anti-gay hysteria in the wake of the Aids epidemic that decimated the population. Mukasa's friends are constantly telling him it is time he got married.

At long last the penny has dropped. Mukasa has begun to sit up and take notice. He has begun to look around him at the young ladies who are still available. He has left it a bit late. Nevertheless, he is persisting in his search and has begun to sign up for dating sites in Kampala.

Recently he met a beautiful young woman at a speed-dating session held at the Hillside Plaza Hotel. He knew immediately she was the right one for him but she did not reciprocate, at least not at first. He has become obsessed with her. He feels confused.

He now has two obsessions: Angel Nandawula and his frogs. He has begun to have really strange dreams in which the two obsessions come together.

For example, he dreamt that he was crossing a road one day near Tank Hill in Kampala when a frog called out to him and said, "If you kiss me, I'll turn into a beautiful princess."

He bent over, picked up the frog and put it in his pocket.

The frog spoke up again and said, "If you kiss me and turn me back into a beautiful princess, I will stay with you for one week."

Mukasa took the frog out of his pocket, smiled at it and put it back in his pocket.

The frog then called out, "If you kiss me and turn me back into a princess, I'll stay with you and do anything, I mean literally anything, you want."

He took the frog out again, smiled at it and put it back into his pocket.

Finally the frog asked, "What is it with you, Mukasa? I've told you I'm a beautiful princess, that I'll stay with you for a week and do anything you want. Why won't you give me a kiss? You keep me in your pocket. It's cruel. Why won't you just drop me back into the ditch so that I can get on with my life?"

In his dream, he remembers himself saying, "Look, I'm a dedicated and professional herpetologist. People look up to me at Bat Valley. I am a leader in my field. I have published thirty articles on herpetology, more, if you count chapters in books. I may even have my own Department of Herpetology soon. I don't have time for girlfriends, but a talking frog is really cool." Mukasa never married.

The Gorilla Man of Bwindi

Alec was a scoutmaster. He was smart. WOSM, the World Organisation of the Scout Movement, had acquired some lucrative estates and was feeling generous. Scout Shops were doing well, as was Scout Insurance Services. An advertisement was placed in *Scout Magazine* offering a grant to anyone wanting to conduct research into the tying of knots.

Alec's attention was drawn to the advert in The Chequers pub in Hendon, a popular watering hole for scoutmasters in North London. He would often be seen there in his shorts, even in winter.

"This is me!" he said to his drinking companions. They all nodded in agreement. He applied and was awarded the money.

Of course, he had to submit a research plan before the full sum could be released. One of the stipulations was that a respected academic had to act as a referee. He had a friend who was lecturing in English at Bat Valley University who signed for him and offered him a desk in his office.

His plan consisted of the following categories: the knot in the English language, the knot in culture, the knot in superstition, the knot in legend, the knot and animals.

Alec's overriding ambition was to visit Africa. The truth was that he was not really interested in knots but he saw in the grant a way of realising his life's dream.

He set about getting the 'easy bit' out of the way. The first chapters rolled off his computer in no time at all.

He described how the ancient Greeks valued the reef knot, which they called 'the knot of Hercules', and how they believed that a bandage tied with this knot would help a wound heal more quickly.

He recorded how Alexander the Great solved the problem

of untying an impossibly complex knot, the Gordian knot, by slashing his sword through it.

He described the significance different knots have for sailors: how some knots were believed to attract a breeze, others a hurricane.

He listed the many references to knots in the English language, 'to tie the knot', 'a knotty problem', 'get knotted' and so on.

He had a solid section on the communication system that involved the tying of knots on cords the Incas called *quipus*. Indeed, he was sorely tempted to spend the money on a trip to Peru but came down in favour of Uganda, mainly because of his friend at the university in Kampala and because of the obsession he had since childhood, to get up close and intimate with a gorilla.

The trustees were happy with his progress and released the full amount of money. He was glad that he had got the boring bits of his research plan out of the way. Now he could concentrate on his main goal. He bought his airline ticket for Africa.

He set about clearing his mind. He had read somewhere that some animals could tie knots, namely the weaver bird and the gorilla. He studied many videos on YouTube of weaver birds constructing their ingenious nests, trying to glimpse the actual tying of a knot with a piece of grass. His aim was to establish what sort of knot they used. None of the films was clear enough. The pictures were taken from a distance.

He knew he had to get up close. His friend at Bat Valley Uni told him that weaver birds, once common in Wandegeya not too far from the university – Wandegeya means the place where weaver birds, *endegeya*, congregate – could be seen in numbers in the trees next to the Lake Victoria hotel in Entebbe. He booked in and set up his video camera. He hired waiters from the hotel to operate the camera while he enjoyed the hotel's marvellous fresh fish dishes.

His heart wasn't in weaver birds. He just couldn't get his

head round them. He had struggled with Carl Gustav Jung's use of them as a metaphor in discussing of archetypes of the unconscious. He couldn't make head nor tail of Jung's theory. Perhaps this had put him off.

No, it was the gorilla he wanted to get to grips with. He was determined to see and possibly film a gorilla tying a knot. He hired a Land Rover and set off for the Bwindi Impenetrable Forest in the south of the country.

He arrived and set up camp. He and his guide Philippe spent days lugging equipment through the trees. He could see how the forest had gained its name. Poachers had been active and recent military conflict had dramatically reduced gorilla numbers. He allowed Philippe to cut a path through the undergrowth.

After three days they were beginning to lose hope of ever even glimpsing a single gorilla let alone observing one tying a knot. He had heard that they secure their nesting places with either a square knot or a granny knot. Granny knots are more frequent.

They found some droppings. The guide put his finger to his lips telling Alec not to make a sound. He indicated with his arm against his head that a gorilla was sleeping just ahead. They went down on all fours, inching their way forward.

Alec got the camera ready. There was a click as he turned it on. The gorilla sat up and looked around sleepily trying to work out where the sound had come from. Alec carried on filming. This was the culminating point of his life. His heart swelled with pride at what he had accomplished. He even felt proud of the way he had hoodwinked the scouting authorities. No matter, he was achieving his life's ambition. He was lying down close to a gorilla. He was doing an Attenborough. It was such an intimate moment.

Suddenly the gorilla caught sight of the lens. It was reflecting the light. He charged as fast as he could towards Alec and the guide. Horrified, they both shot up. Philippe swung round and stuck his elbow in Alec's eye, knocking him out. Alec

54

slumped to the ground. The gorilla stopped just inches away from them.

All that Alec could show for his labours when he got back to London was a beautiful black eye. He went before the panel to explain what he had found. His story didn't ring true. They felt that he had pulled the wool over their eyes. He had blotted his copybook. He was asked to leave the movement.

The Gower Hippo Boy

Bob was an Egyptologist. He was from a village near Swansea. He became interested in hippopotami when he was a small child. His house was near Paviland Cave in Gower. Readers will have heard of the Red Lady of Paviland. In addition to the bones of the red lady - who, it appears now, was a man whose redness was the result, probably, of the action of natural chemicals in the soil - those of lions, tigers, elephants, hippos and other animals now extinct, were also found.

He was fascinated by the fact that the bones of 'African' animals had been found not much more than a stone's throw from his bedroom. It thrilled him to picture herds of hippos moving across the land, now sea, between his cliffs and those of England in the distance, across the present-day Bristol Channel, then savannah. The sill of his window, facing the sea, had several model hippos on it. He went dressed as a hippo to fancy dress parties held at his local primary school. "A hippopot am I" he would joke, trying to scare the girls. He was called 'The Hippo Boy' at Knelston County Primary School.

He eventually graduated from the Department of Egyptology, University College, London. He had taken early retirement and was now attached to the Egypt Centre at Swansea University. His title there was Honorary Lecturer in Ancient History and Egyptology. He went out to Africa to conduct research into religion in Africa. He was working with Dr Aziz of The Department of Religion and Peace Studies at Bat Valley. He had landed an enormous grant from the government of Qatar.

He began his studies in Egypt. In fact, he had become totally absorbed in one aspect of ancient Egyptian culture in particular: the deification of the hippopotamus.

56

"But there are no hippos in Egypt!" one difficult Swansea academic had scoffed dismissively during a paper he had delivered in the Egypt Centre.

"Ah, but there were," Bob replied. "Egypt was teeming with hippos back then. Their number was so great that royal families organised hippo hunts on the Nile. These hunts would underline the divinity of the kings. The creatures caused such chaos trampling crops at night in the fields lining the river, that their numbers had to be controlled."

Bob's paper was met with polite applause.

He spent a great deal of time in the British Museum in London and in The Egyptian Museum of Cairo. He combed the souks and bazaars of that great city looking for objects connected with the hippo cult. His collection of magic wands, carved from hippo ivory, used in the past to calm and control rampant hippos, was his pride and joy.

He rummaged around in the antique shops of Alexandria, Port Said, Luxor and Aswan in his search for rare objects, specifically Tawaret amulets. Tawaret was the protective Egyptian goddess of women in childbirth. She was depicted as a two-legged female hippopotamus with cat-like attributes, pendulous breasts and the back of a Nile crocodile.

The worship of Tawaret, he discovered, percolated down to Nubia (northern Sudan and southern Egypt). Bob had accumulated a considerable collection of clay statuettes of the goddess, fakes of course, but he didn't mind.

Tawaret, he would argue, could be described as apotropaic. The word means to turn away, to ward off harm, misfortune - even the evil eye. In the case of the Nile, one problem was excessive flooding. She and objects associated with her were used as one attempt to mitigate this. It was a complicated process. A balance had to be struck. Sediment from the Blue Nile, that flows out of Lake Tana in Ethiopia, is what kept Egypt alive. It still does. In order to persuade the gods to continue to cause the floods, the pharaoh, with great ceremony, would perform very strange rituals on the Nile.

Tawaret was put to all sort of uses, he discovered. Household objects would be designed in her image. Bob had several vessels in her shape used, it was thought, in an attempt to purify drinking water. Liquid would be poured through her nipples. Bob loved using these objects in his talks. He used one as water jug on his table.

He gradually worked his way down the Nile. He realised that hippopotami had once been common sights from Cairo to the Cape. Now, he perceived, they were concentrated mainly in certain areas of sub-Saharan Africa.

He began to write a book about his findings: *The Hippopotamus* by Robert Beynon. He used the Sudan Library for a while. He really enjoyed his chapter on Tawaret, the protector of women in childbirth. Deep down she reminded him of an aunt who had looked after him for several years in Swansea. He described how the ancients had observed how well female hippos looked after their young. He had photos of hippos carrying their young on their backs and films of them suckling their infants under water.

He moved south to Kampala. His office at Bat Valley University became popular with students. They relished his stories and the objects he had collected. Bob really loved his research area. It had become all-consuming. He thought about it day and night. Anything he could find in the Bat Valley University library about hippos intrigued him. He was delighted to discover there that there was a Hippopotamus clan in Buganda, called the *Nvubu*.

His book grew by leaps and bounds. In it he wrote that there were numerous clans (at least fifty) in Buganda: the *Ennyange* - the Cattle Egret; the *Nvuma* - Pearl; the *Njovu* - Elephant; the *Nkula* - Rhinoceros; the *Kinyomi* - Ant; the *Ngaali* - Crested Crane; the *Nojobi* - Marsh Antelope and, of course, the *Nvubu* - the Hippopotamus. His book included interviews with hippopotamus clan members.

He visited reverently Mbazi hill on the Kojja Peninsula on which Kyaaggwe was established. Roughly half-way between

Kampala and Jinja, it is said to be the seat of the clan. He fell in love with the mystique of the place and had had a small house built there where he spent most of his time.

He noted how the clan had been in charge of the large canoes of the king. He discovered that they paddled the Kabaka's boats wherever he wanted to go. They made bracelets and anklets for the King's wives. Their drum was the *Ntamviva*. Their duties all centred on Lake Nnalubaale (Lake Victoria).

According to the myth, they had chosen both the tortoise and hippopotamus as totems following an incident when Kayita, their founder, was born. The afterbirth was a tortoise that grew into a hippopotamus. In addition, Kayita had lost his son Kaseeseeba to a hippo on the lake. In his anger and grief, he ordered his children to approach the hippo with extreme care. Occupying so much of their attention, it eventually became their totem, the spirit and symbol that represented and watched over their clan.

Bob felt he had gone full circle. His journey had taken him from protective wands and amulets at the top of the Nile down to the hippo as protector near the source of that great river. His book was taking shape nicely.

Bob's life had profound meaning, a meaning bestowed on it by the hippopotamus and his research on it. To him, rather than being the ugliest of creatures, it was incredibly beautiful. It may have been the way it was linked with a feminine Nile deity but he actually began to prefer the look of women with huge legs. There was something sensual about the hippo's legs. Instead of Job's behemoth, thought by many to have been a hippo, he saw something elegant, warm and protective. He loved even their flat feet with their four webbed toes. It still blew his mind that they could support a weight of five tons.

It was with these thoughts that he ventured out one starlit night onto the bank of Lake Victoria. He had been socialising in Kisumu Club after a rugby match. Bob loved contact sports, the clash of bodies on the field. Outside, under the stars, he felt at one with the world, especially with Uganda.

He was found the next day face down in the mud. He had panicked the hippos that were grazing on the shore. They all rushed into the water when they heard him coming. He had been flattened. His lifeless body was as flat as a pancake.

The Jaguar Men of Kiziba

There are no jaguars in Africa, I hear you say. Wrong. I knew of one.

Phil was a character. He was unconventional. Jean Baptiste was from Rwanda. They both taught French at a school in a tiny village near Kampala called Kiziba. Jean also prided himself on being unconventional but envied Phil's more extreme unconventionality.

Phil had bought the King of Rwanda's car. He had beaten it into the shape of a bullet. Jean dreamt of driving it around Kampala. It became an obsession.

When Phil first heard about the car, he knew that he had to buy it. A friend rang to say that had seen a beautiful old car on a piece of wasteland next to a palm tree garage-cum-dump. It took a long time for Phil to locate the owner, a diplomat, between forty and fifty, overweight, with an unhealthy complexion. He told Phil that he and some fellow Belgians had escaped from Rwanda in the vehicle and that it was one of the last King of Rwanda's fleet. It was a grey Jaguar Mk 5 coupé, 4.2 litres, with a podium behind the front seat for the king to stand on whenever he wanted to wave at his subjects.

One day, Phil had to go back to London. Jean saw his opportunity.

The car had no papers. Phil had used it for a year with false number plates and a forged window sticker. The new government had started enforcing 'The Dangerous Mechanical Condition' law. If Phil had been caught, he would have lost his licence and the car. These would only have been returned after an inspection. Jean didn't know any of this. He didn't even have a licence. The steering was dangerously worn. There was about three quarters of a turn of slack on the steering wheel and it had no insurance. There would have been serious consequences if

61

the police had stopped him.

All of this coincided with a visit to Uganda by Princess Margaret.

Putting on Phil's best suit and placing his friend's top hat carefully on the passenger seat, Jean drove away down the unpaved road towards the city. He felt that the banana trees were waving at him as he went by. He drove around the city but found that many of the streets had been closed off so that the visiting royal could be driven straight to the Governor's house. At a roadblock a policeman mistook the car for the royal conveyance and waved him onto the royal route! Jean drove slowly along the crowd-lined route, wrestling with the wheel, while thousands of people cheered and waved flags.

As he approached Bat Valley University, Jean waved at the awe-struck crowds. They waved back confused. They were expecting a princess. Instead they saw a person who, with his fine Tustsi features, looked like their King, the Kabaka of Buganda. Jean stopped, stood on the podium, and waved regally at his 'subjects'.

Feeling ecstatic, he decided that it was time to head back. He looked for a back road. He did not know that there was a problem with one of the carburettors (the car had three). The faulty one started spraying gallons of petrol on to the side of the engine and all around under the bonnet. The engine became slightly sluggish. He could hear the fuel pump on the petrol tank ticking fast. He didn't know that, normally, Phil would stop the car and tap the carburettor in a particular way in order to fix it.

On the way back down the red murram road, its surface like corrugated iron strewn with ball bearings, the car's engine burst into flames, scorching the banana trees on either side of the road. The car carried on hurtling along in a ball of flames, filling the air with thick black smoke until, finally, it crashed into a tree.

Jean was already dead when the villagers arrived at the scene.

The Lungfish Man of Mbazi

Charles was a visionary. He had his eye on the future. Scientists were at last discussing the possibility of Humanity spreading out to other planets, even to other galaxies.

He had just come back from a conference on interplanetary travel in London. Two ideas had caught his imagination. One involved the creation of massive disks that could create 'light sails' that would propel very heavy space ships at tremendous speed between stars. So far, it was argued, it would only be possible if one could harvest light using a disk the size of three Earths. One astronomer claimed that technically superior beings had already mastered the technology. There were beeps, energy surges, he said, coming from outer space that could only be explained in this way.

The other idea that had fired his imagination involved the lungfish. Lungfish can not only survive out of water, they can hide in mud and go into suspended animation during periods of drought. They are found all over Uganda. Lungfish fishermen have pockmarked the countryside with small pools in which they breed them.

The lungfish market was beginning to boom. The taboo according to which women were not allowed to eat lungfish was beginning to fade. Some had argued that the taste of lungfish was too strong for women.

Now, as anyone in Buganda will tell you, the Lungfish Clan is powerful. Charles managed to get himself invited to a gathering of the clan at the Kololo Gardens Hotel. The event was held to launch the idea of a state-of-the–art heritage centre at Njajja. Tickets were on sale at one hundred thousand shillings, well over a hundred dollars. It was worth it for he met some important Chinese investors who said they would help.

The Lungfish or Mamba Clan is the largest in Buganda with more than three million members. They are, it is said, the first clan to modernise, to bring its norms and customs into the twentieth century. Other clans in Buganda are watching their progress with great interest. In the presence of Lungfish Clan people you can feel Buganda beginning to heal after a long period of disaster for their culture.

The Mamba Clan has many outstanding members, ranging from the fields of sport, politics and commerce to the church. They have produced nine Kabakas, including Mwanga I, Suuna II, Kiwewa, and Kalema. In the past the admiral of the Kabaka's navy was always a chief of the Mamba - Lungfish Clan.

Now, the lungfish can be found in Lake Victoria, in swamps, in rice fields and in the holes mentioned above. It is renowned for its ability to survive. There are stories of lungfish getting set inside mud bricks. These can sit in a wall until the right rain triggers their revival. They can then wriggle out of the wall onto the floor.

It can sleep for five years without taking sustenance. It seems that they slow down their biological clock. The fish produce very little waste during hibernation and use practically no energy. Current thinking is that their secret lies in their genes.

Charles set about trying to identify them. His research was going well. He was linked online with scientists all over the world: China, Russia, the USA, the UK, France, any country with a space programme.

The billionaires Elon Musk, Jeff Bezos and Richard Branson were showing interest. If Charles could isolate the Lungfish's survival gene, could it be introduced into humans? Things were looking promising.

As many researchers will tell you, there is a danger that you can take your work - and yourself - too seriously. At least, that is how some feel. As a result practical jokes are often played. One of Charles's assistants was a bit of a joker.

A delegation from the Lungfish clan dropped in on him unexpectedly. His laboratory was a mess. In the very centre of the room lay a live lungfish. It had a lighted cigarette in its mouth. Cries of outrage greeted the sight.

Charles tried to explain that a colleague was trying to see if lungfish could get lung cancer. It was not true. He only dug himself deeper into the hole. The damage had been done.

A letter reached the Vice-Chancellor. Two days later Charles was called in. He was hauled over the coals. He was told in no uncertain terms that the joke had gone down very badly with everybody at the highest levels in the university. (Some of his colleagues had almost split their sides laughing.) Charles explained it was the work of a rogue assistant.

It was decided that he should go to MIT, the Massachusetts Institute of Technology in Cambridge, Massachusetts.

"It's an ill wind that blows no good", he said to himself, sitting back to sip his first glass of champagne as the jet taking him to America took off low over Lake Victoria.

The Mount Elgon Waiter

They were a close group of friends. Thrown together by circumstances, and each coming from a different class background, they formed an unbreakable band of brothers and sisters. They were there to help the country move from being a protectorate to an independent nation.

They went everywhere together, exploring the emerging nations outside the one in which they were based: Uganda.

One night they found themselves erecting a tent near Lake Manyara, in Tanzania. The place is called Mto wa Mbu. Their Swahili was still elementary. It means Mosquito River. They rolled down the windows to let some air in. Within seconds a swarm of mosquitoes flew into the tent. The rest of the night was spent round the log fire.

They beat a hasty retreat north to Kenya. It was the holidays. They had no fixed plans. They made for Amboseli game park. It was getting dark when they arrived so they decided to spend the night in the car.

Once bitten, twice shy. Dave, from West Wales, warned everyone not to open the windows. They fell asleep. A little while later Dave awoke to a familiar whining in his ear. His face was covered in mosquitoes!

"Who opened the window?" he shouted.

"It was getting too stuffy," said Cathy.

The only satisfaction Dave gained from the experience was that she ended up with numerous bites, whereas he escaped unscathed.

The car, a green Ford Zephyr 4, was scoured for mosquitoes. The decision was made to move on and they made their way back to Uganda.

Still in Kenya, they found themselves driving through a

wood. The sun was high. The car started filling up again with flies. This time they were larger than the ones that had attacked them the night before. They all agreed that they looked like horse flies.

"We call them 'brims' in Gower, Dave said, rather randomly.

"Fly farasi here," said Basil. Nobody could gainsay him.

"What's that?" cried Jane, pointing at an old wooden sign. They stopped the car and reversed the car to read it.

In big capital letters, it said **'TSE-TSE FLY AREA'**.

They drove as quickly as they could towards Uganda.

Night was coming on. They were near Awoja Swamp, not far from Soroti. Kate wanted to see some wild life and the lilies. They took a track and parked. It was now too late to pitch the tent. This time they checked to see that all the windows were closed.

Basil got out to answer a call of nature. On his return, half asleep, he failed to close the door properly. He remembers closing it gently so as not to wake the others up. The courtesy light stayed on all night. The following morning the car was full of bloated mosquitoes. There were so many, it was like a thick smog in the car.

Feeling wretched and fearing the worst, they made for the Mount Elgon Hotel in nearby Soroti.

"This'll cost an arm and a leg," said Cathy dejectedly.

Nobody replied. They were a sorry sight as they traipsed in, faces bright red with bites. It took them all morning to straighten themselves out.

After showers and a rest they made for the dining room. They sat down with a sigh of relief as they saw the lush, deep pile carpet, the chandelier, the red tablecloth, the napkins placed like little pyramids, the silver-plated cutlery, the sparkling wine glasses and the bottle of French wine already opened. Dave had rung down to order it. He always insisted on his wine being *chambré*. It was a thing he had picked up at the Fairyhill Restaurant in Gower.

They sat down and reached for their napkins. An immaculately dressed waiter brought the soup. It was *Soupe à l'oignon gratinée traditionnelle.* Basil had ordered it earlier with the wine. He had a soft spot for Kate. She had worked *as an assistante de langue anglaise* in Paris prior to coming to Uganda to work as an English teacher.

They all beamed at the waiter who said, "Mesdames, messieurs", as he bowed and withdrew from their table backwards. They began to savour the onions. Dave said that he could taste a good white wine in the soup.

Suddenly Basil blurted out, "What the heck!"

Everybody in the restaurant turned round to see what the commotion was about. Basil was peering into his soup.

"Shush!" whispered Kate. She hated public scenes and would do anything to avoid them. Jane looked round at the other guests with an embarrassed grin.

"Leave it," said Dave. "It won't kill you."

"I am sorry," said Basil loudly. "If I am paying this much for a meal, I don't expect to come across this."

He held up an object with his fork. The waiters came out from the kitchen. The chefs were peering through the round window in the door behind them.

"Waiter," Basil bellowed, crimson with rage. "Come here."

"Yes, sir?"

"There's a mosquito in my soup."

The waiter came across. He was not at all happy with Basil's manner. He looked Basil up and down, weighing him up, pointedly taking in the crumpled and rather soiled clothes. "Old colonial type from Kenya," he thought.

Basil, annoyed at the waiter's silence, shouted, "Fetch the manager immediately".

"I can't, sir."

"What do you mean, you can't? This is outrageous!"

"That *is* the manager, sir. The last customer was a witch doctor!"

The Moth Lady of Tororo

I was on my way back to Kampala, having attended the funeral of a rancher friend of mine who had just been shot dead in Kenya. An MP was under suspicion of having instigated the events that led up to his murder. An army of ten thousand herdsmen, desperate for fresh grazing land, had been invading nature conservancy areas, ranches and smallholdings in Laikipia, north of Nairobi.

I was upset. I had lost a friend. I drove my Mercedes Benz into the car park of the Rock Classic Hotel in Tororo, just over the border from Kenya. I made for my favourite place near the swimming pool and ordered an ice-cold lager.

She saw me arrive. She carried on swimming, pretending not to have seen me. She climbed out, slipped into a multi-coloured robe and sat down at the table next to mine. I noticed there was a Fanta on it.

"You look a bit down in the mouth," she said.

"Oh, yes, we have just buried a good friend in Kenya," I replied. "I am on my way back to Kampala."

"Oh," she said, "I have just completed a study of the moths in the Turkana area of northern Kenya."

"Bit dry up there for moths," I said.

"I was working out of the Turkana Basin Institute, you know, Richard Leakey's brainchild. Are you interested in moths?"

"Yes," I replied. "At night my garden high up on a hillside in Kampala is full of them. There are some wonderful ones. I have a big house with an enormous garden full of exotic flowers that attract the moths at night: Night Jasmine, Gardenia, Honeysuckle, that sort of thing."

She pulled her chair closer.

"I stopped off," she said, "in western Kenya to study the Tent Moths and the beautiful sheets of silk that their caterpillars spread over the trees. Saw lots of hawk moths. Actually I am on my way back to Kampala too."

"Ah!"

"Yes."

"I am doing a PhD at Bat Valley University."

"Oh!"

"Yes."

My mind is racing. I am getting on in years. Is she just feeling lonely and being polite to an older man? What can I call her? I know, I'll call her 'The Moth'. Moths are attracted to bright lights in the dark. I am beginning feel less sorry for myself.

"What are you investigating in Uganda?" I asked politely.

"My research there has a witchcraft dimension. I am trying to establish the place of the moth in local superstitions."

"How interesting!" I lied.

She had shaken off her robe and was leaning back in her chair to let her bikini dry. I couldn't help admiring her.

I rummaged around in the drawers of my mind for something to say.

"We called moths 'witches' in Gower," I said.

"Gower?" she asked.

"You know, Dylan Thomas's backyard when he was a youngster. I am from Llangennith at the far end of the peninsula."

"Oh!"

I needed to up my game. Why would she be interested in the Gower Peninsula?

"I remember a conversation I had with an old farmer. I wrote it down and published it in a book. I can remember it so clearly."

"Go on," she said.

"He was alone. A moth was fluttering against his oil lamp.

'We call them witches,' he whispered.

'Witches?' I repeated.

'Yes, witches,' he said.

'Moths come out at night. Witches come out at night?'

'Yes,' he breathed.

'Moths undergo metamorphosis, witches can transform themselves into cats?'

'That's what some used to say,' he murmured.

'Moths fly by night. Witches fly by night?'

'Yes.'

'Witches have long noses. Moths have long noses?'

'Perhaps,' he replied with a faint smile.

'Do you believe in witches?' I asked him.

'Don't be ridiculous!' he cried."

I wished immediately that I had not included that last line.

"Very good!" she said, clapping her hands enthusiastically. "Not all witches are ugly, you know."

This last comment troubled me.

"Tell me more about your research," I said.

She reached for her rucksack and took out a notebook.

"You won't believe what I found a couple of months ago. I met this chap who works as a witch doctor. He claims he can predict the future. He is very popular in Kampala. I wrote down what he said. There's masses of stuff. I'll select just one piece. Listen to this:

I was looking through the curtains to see what my neighbour was having for breakfast. A moth floated down onto one of the curtains and began to speak. I wrote down the moth's words:

The country's football team will get new boots from a very rich man with a lot of money and shades. So wealthy, he'll wear garments made out of 50,000 Uganda Shilling notes. The team will rise to new heights with its new football boots, and they'll go on to win glory throughout the continent of Africa."

"Brilliant," I said, not knowing quite how to respond. She looked at me intently as if she was trying to read my thoughts. I began to feel slightly uneasy.

71

Suddenly she said, "Would you like to see my moth collection?"

"Wh .. where?" I stuttered. "At Bat Valley?"

"No upstairs in my room."

I picked up my glass and knocked back what remained of its contents. She took this as a sign that I was interested and got up. She turned to go and I saw a moth tattoo on her back. It was the first time I had seen it.

"That's a beautiful image on your back," I said.

I couldn't bring myself to say tattoo. I am not keen on tattoos.

"What is it?" I asked.

"It's a vampire moth. They suck blood, you know. Their proboscis can penetrate the skin of a buffalo." She grinned. "Coming?"

"Can I take a rain check?" I said. "I have a difficult case to prepare tomorrow in the High Court."

"Please yourself," she said, miffed. She clearly wasn't used to being turned down. There was an awkward moment. Neither she nor I knew what to say.

"Must fly!" she said.

(Author's note: the above story was recorded on the terrace of a bar on Kampala Road. It is reproduced here with the person in question's permission.)

The Kampala Shopping Mall Ostrich Man

I t is difficult to describe Paul. He has lectured in Art in Africa for almost the whole of his working life. Physically he is rather unattractive. He is very tall and has a small head. His neck is long. Some of the students call him 'Rubberneck'. Some colleagues call him 'The Ostrich'.

Paul has survived in Uganda through thick and thin. His technique is simply to ignore what is happening. He breezes along without being ruffled by what may be happening. When reality begins to impinge on him, metaphorically he buries his head in the sand.

The only thing that ruffled his feathers was the looting of Drapers House. He loved the 'antiquity' of Drapers. The building, still there, dates from the early 1930s. The robbery had upset him, as had the looting of Kampala's first supermarket, Cashco, behind Drapers House, stripped bare by looters in 1979 in the wake of the Liberation war.

Paul is not perfect. Like most of us, he has, what he calls, 'a naughty side'. He likes flirting with the ladies.

His pastime is shopping. At least, that is what he claims. It is what he tells his wife and his son. She will often go with him - she has her suspicions perhaps. The truth is that Paul feels that it is easy for him to approach women, to chat them up, while out shopping. He likes to hang around the freezers in supermarkets while his wife goes wandering off. He strikes up conversations with ladies doing their weekly shop.

He has numerous chat-up lines, some of them border-line risky. If he feels that giving his targets the glad eye is beginning to misfire, he takes refuge in a joke, such as the following one.

This actually happened in the new Mega Standard six-storeyed supermarket in Kampala.

He caught the eye of an extremely beautiful Rwandan woman examining the apples in the fruit area. At first she smiled back at him. He drew near. She shot him a disapproving look. He had misjudged the situation. He adopted his familiar fall-back position:

"I've lost my wife here in the supermarket. Can you talk to me for a couple of minutes?"

The tall, traditionally dressed lady looked puzzled.

"Why should I talk to you?" she asked.

"Because whenever I talk to a woman with eyes like yours, my wife appears out of nowhere."

The young woman laughed and he laughed. No harm was done and they both went on their way.

And so it goes on. His wife knows he is doing it but she has become resigned to his wandering eye. After all, she argues, no real damage is being done. Their marriage appears to be safe. He is still with her. "He's all mouth and no trousers", she tells her friends.

Anyway, that's what she seems to think. From time to time Paul will hit the jackpot. He will actually meet somebody who is flattered by his attention.

He struck gold in the Kasumba Square Mall. It lies at the intersection of Busega Roundabout and the Northern Bypass. There is a guest-house there for the shopper who needs - how can I put it? - to find somewhere to rest his or her head.

Nobody can understand how he does it. He is far from being God's gift to women. The generally held theory is that he manages to impress his conquests by introducing them to his hobby. This may sound unbelievable, until you hear what it is. He is obsessed with ostriches, their habits, their speed (in races), their eggs, their feathers, their meat, everything.

He invites his ladies to a meal at The Lawns Restaurant in Impala Avenue, Kololo. He dangles the enticing menu before their eyes: Impala, Kudu, Springbok, Wildebeest, Crocodile Tail and, the *pièce de résistance*, Ostrich.

He invites them to his office at the university to inspect his collection of decorated ostrich eggs. Many of them are breathtakingly beautiful. They had been painted with elephants, zebras, maps of Africa, crested cranes, orthodox religious icons and of course, ostriches. He encourages his students to paint the eggs.

That is Paul, a complex character perhaps and difficult to like when you know how he conducts his life. On the one hand, he is oblivious to major events going on around him - he carried on regardless, kept his head down, during the atrocious Amin years - on the other hand, he is hyper-aware of the vulnerability of some women. Well, 'Let him [or her] that is without sin cast the first stone'.

He has a side-line. It's how he finances his philandering. He supplies ostrich feathers to the hat industry in Luton, England. He can be seen from time to time putting boxes of feathers through customs at Entebbe. He takes charge of the dyeing and is immensely proud of his white, red, orange, yellow, blue, indigo and violet products. The Art syllabus covers dyeing.

Feathers that are not up to being placed in the exotic hats worn by the ladies at the races at Royal Ascot are put to another purpose. A lucrative side-line to the first side-line - his salary has not kept up with the cost of living - are his ostrich feather dusters. He has a small lock-up in Kampala where he employs a man to fix the feathers on a stick. His gets his supplies from an ostrich farm to the south of Masaka. His businesses are going well in a Uganda that has enjoyed stability since the nineteen-eighties.

Things nearly came apart at the seams recently. He was standing in a queue at a supermarket in Garden City when he noticed an attractive Muganda woman behind him. She had just raised her hand and was smiling broadly. She was saying hello.

"Osiibye otya nno, ssebo" [Good afternoon], she said.

He was rather taken aback that such a fine-looking woman

would be waving at him, and although her face was vaguely familiar, he couldn't place where he might have known her from.

"Sorry, do you know me?" he said.

"I may be mistaken, but I thought you might be the father of one of my children," she replied.

Paul's mind shot back to the times he had been unfaithful.

"Oh!" he said, "Did we meet on Trev's stag do in Entebbe?"

She looked puzzled.

"When I got out of the police station and got back to the hotel room you had gone," he said.

He looked round to see if anyone was listening. He saw his wife and son approaching. Perspiration began to seep through his shirt.

"No," she replied, "I'm your son's Geography teacher".

The Owl Man of Mukono

Keith was sitting comfortably preparing his lecture for the following Monday. He had just eaten a huge pile of cauliflower cheese prepared for him by his Congolese 'home help'. The sun was setting, casting patches of gold on the wall behind him. Up there in his flat at Bat Valley University he felt that all was right with the world.

Keith had studied owls in Patagonia before coming to Bat Valley. He had lived there at a troubled time in Argentina's history. He had witnessed terrible things. A doctor had advised him to get treated for something he was suffering from, akin to PTSD. He told him to 'self-medicate' by putting down on paper any tell-tale signs of his illness. He wrote this down after one particularly troubling dream. He liked to use a prose poem format for this type of activity.

> *"I am a child in a wood of lenga trees - a sort of beech.*
> *We are next to a river in which we are fishing.*
> *Some one is carving the letters of a name, 'Luciana',*
> *into the bark of a tree.*
> *The river is called 'Olivia'.*
> *It is a river that is formed from the melting snow*
> *of Monte Olivia near Ushuaia.*
> *It is good sitting here catching rainbow trout.*
> *One of the group stands up, stares and points.*
> *No one knows what is wrong but we all look.*
> *We can see a tall, dark, browny-black creature.*
> *It has red eyes, with pointed ears on top of its head.*
> *It seems to be a cross between a man, a bird and a bear.*
> *It starts gliding towards us, seemingly levitating on*
> *yellow light.*

We start to run, but it seems impossible.
It is as if we are being pulled back towards it.
We run out of the wood into a meadow.
As we run across the grass we can see a yellow glow.
It is staying within the trees, skirting round the field.
It is travelling fast.
It's a race between us going across the field
and it, going all the way round.
We get to the other side and enter a large tunnel
that goes under a motorway leading to Ushuaia.
The far side of the tunnel is blocked by a grill.
There is a gap just big enough for us to slip through.
We all get through, we keep running.
We hear the iron grate rattling behind us.
There is a terrible screech echoing in the tunnel.
That night, from my window,
I see a light rise up in the sky
and zoom off in a flash.
There seem to be things dropping from it.
They look like bodies falling into the sea."

Keith had never really tried to analyse that dream. He knew it was trying to tell him something but he was too lazy to uncover what. It just sat there in a notebook in his desk.

Curiously, it seems that he developed there, in Patagonia, mild oclaphobia, a fear of owls. As can seen from the above dream, he had tried to analyse why this had happened. One of his theories was that he had been affected by blood-curdling stories in Latin America that linked owls with witches. He vowed to himself never to mention this link with witchcraft in his lectures at the BVU. He felt it would go down badly with his peers.

The title of his forthcoming lecture was 'The Owls of Uganda'. He wrote this note:

"The Verreaux's Eagle-Owl has a whitish face, shaped like an oval disk with a black border and it has two feather tufts on

78

its head."

He took a sip of beer.

"Its feathers are light grey below and dark brown on top."

He stretched his legs out in front of him and yawned.

A cloud came into his mind. He had to go and see his in-laws at the weekend. He didn't totally enjoy visiting them but his Mugandan wife always insisted that he drove her there. He liked their house and he did enjoy staying there in some ways, even though he preferred his bed in the flat at the university. His in-laws' hut had no windows, just large openings that you could climb in and out of. He had mixed feelings about being there.

Something bothered him about one of his father-in-law's three wives, the eldest. It was the way that she was made to sleep in a small thatched hut at the bottom of the *shamba* - the small plot behind the main hut. He had often wondered why they did that. He had concluded, without much conviction, that it was a throw-back to the past, when old folk could be suffering from incurable diseases. He had never been able to ask his wife why they did it.

Anyway, it was an experience going there. His father-in-law had taught him how to fire his old Enfield rifle. Many Baganda had hunting rifles in their homes then.

"The best place in Uganda to find Verreaux's Eagle-Owl is in Semliki National Park," he wrote. Surely the students would know that already, he thought. The lecture preparation was going badly. He put his hands behind his head and looked up at the ceiling.

"Ah, the Semliki Safari Lodge in the Toro-Semliki Wildlife Reserve!" he sighed. He loved going there and sitting under the thatch by the pool sipping a cool Nile. He adored the log cabin effect of the building. Semliki bush breakfasts, served at a table where you could sit and absorb nature, were his idea of heaven. He was beginning to prefer game lodges to the animals.

"You can see Verreaux's Eagle-Owls roosting in the tall trees at Semliki," he jotted down.

He took another sip of his beer. Florence, his home-help/cook/general factotum asked him if he wanted another bottle from the fridge. "Yes," he nodded.

"They can weigh up to almost half a stone and their wingspan is almost seven feet," he scribbled.

"Boring," he thought. "I'll have to jazz it up."

He wrote: "Verreaux's Eagle-Owls can eat thorny hedgehogs. In South Africa you can find piles of hedgehog skins next to their nests. They skin their prey alive…. It has bright pink eyelids."

Keith sat back and sighed as he put his biro down. It was almost dark. He got out of his chair and packed a few things for the weekend. He picked his wife up outside the Faculty office. She kept a change of clothing at her parents' home.

It was dark by the time they drove up the narrow mud road that leads to the house near Mukono. Keith was already drowsy but readily accepted his father-in-law's kind offer of a cold Tusker. It was not long before he took to his bed. He knew that alcohol could give him nightmares but he was weak-willed.

He lay there on the bed, trying to fall asleep. He heard an owl screeching. The noise was eerie, nerve-racking. It went on and on. He no longer knew if he was awake or asleep. He told his wife the next day that he hadn't been able to stand the noise a second longer. He grabbed his father-in-law's rifle off the wall and went outside, waiting for the screeching to start again. As if acting automatically, he raised the rifle and fired into the tree from where the screech was coming. The owl dropped down onto the ground with an horrendous cry. He went back to bed and slept the sleep of the just.

Early the next morning he went out to inspect the dead owl. There under a banana tree lay the body of an old lady. A small crowd had formed. He heard someone utter the word "witch?". The corpse was that of the eldest of his father-in-law's wives. He had shot his mother-in-law!

The Bat Valley University
Mantis Man

W e were at an art gallery in London, standing in front of M. C. Escher's 'Dream' and staring at the praying mantis.* He was on holiday from Bat Valley where he lectured in Biology and where we had met. He was an authority on the Praying Mantis. I had obtained a very temporary post at Goldsmiths where I had been asked to cover for a lecturer in Art who was on maternity leave.

"I always found them creepy in Kampala," I commented.

"I had several Praying Mantis in Uganda and Hong Kong," he began. "With huge eyes situated on its triangular head, the mantis has superb vision. To add to your impression of 'creepiness', if you first gained their attention with a finger moved across their vision, the head would gradually turn and follow the movement of your finger. One could almost believe, at that point, that there was a reasoning being behind that mechanical exterior."

He paused to peer more closely at the painting.

"Each eye is composed of several thousand individual facets, each acting as a separate eye, so that the vision comprises a myriad images, each slightly different from each other and giving depth. Their absolute immobility when stalking prey gives a mantis camouflage whilst the moving prey drifting across their vision is highlighted as a progressive three-dimensional image so that the final lunge is unerring, trapping the victim in those huge spiny front limbs. If the prey has any feelings whatsoever, spare a thought as the mantis mechanically and unemotionally chomps into its body, held totally immobile. I loved to watch them feed on locusts in the Bat Valley laboratory."

He paused then went on again.

"One alarming fact is that the male mantis approaches the female – normally twice or more in size - with great care and caution. And well he might as, in a final gesture, the female eventually allows copulation and then promptly devours him. A perfect analogy to humans, from my experience."

"Yes, I am sorry about that," I replied.

He looked sad. I knew whom he was thinking about. I didn't like to ask him about her. I had always wanted to ask him about the Lebanon that he knew so well and where he had met her but it was a no-go area.

"Let's look at this picture here," I added, trying to change the subject. "It shows a bishop or an abbot wearing a mitre, stretched out on a catafalque. Is he dead? Is he praying? One only lies on a catafalque during, before or after a funeral. His hands are folded like those of a corpse. His eyes are closed. He could be sleeping. The drawing in black and white gives him an ashen, lifeless pallor."

My friend drew nearer to the picture.

"The buildings around the body and the mantis," I went on, "seem to be coming apart. The bishop's world and his power are disappearing. The mystery of the dark universe beyond the bishop's palace that seems to be floating in space is beckoning."

My friend was now peering closely at the details.

"What is it about the Praying Mantises?" I continued. "Why have they always fascinated me? I sometimes thought it was the name itself that intrigued me. Is it spelt 'Praying' with an 'a' or 'Preying', with an 'e'?

He looked at me strangely.

"Why juxtapose a bishop with an insect? Is the insect about to make love? Escher certainly seems to be playing with the pun 'praying and preying'. Its claws are raised in prayer. They also seem to be on the point of devouring the body on which it is kneeling."

"Are preying and praying a pun in Dutch?" my friend asked.

"I don't know," I replied. "I don't think so."

"The details are very precise," he whispered. There was no one else left in the gallery.

"Is he saying," I asked, "that bishops who prey on the souls of the faithful are on the way out, no longer relevant? Is the drawing anti-clerical? That thought too makes me uneasy."

"The creature's taxonomic name, *Mantis religiosa*, means 'religious mantis'," my friend volunteered.

"Ah," I added, "Escher is linking the two, the bishop and the insect, via a pun. *Catafalco* in Italian means scaffolding as well as catafalque. The scaffolding that supports the cleric is disintegrating. I'm beginning to get it."

"In Spanish *catafalco*," my friend said, "can mean a cenotaph."

How did he know that? I remembered he had once lived in Mallorca.

"How can the mantis eat a man of stone?" I asked.

There was no reply.

Digging deeper, he replied, "Mantids belong to the insect order Mantodea and Mantodea comes from the Greek word μάντις (pronounced mantis) meaning prophet. Escher's mantis is not dead but the bishop looks as if he is. The insect's look is triumphal. It has won."

"Good point," I agreed. The end of religious prophecies about the future?

"Could be," he nodded.

Then I said, as if having a revelation, "But it's called 'The Dream'! The picture isn't real. The death isn't real. The mantis is only alive in a dream. What does the dream mean? Are the various levels of meaning we have detected its overall meaning?"

"It isn't a dream," he replied. "It's just called that. Dream is used here as a device to explore some ideas."

"Is Escher depicting a dream he had or is he asking us to ask if the bishop is dreaming about the mantis?" I asked.

We were tying ourselves in knots. Perhaps that was

Escher's intention.

"The mantis looks triumphant," I observed. "Is this picture a reference to destructive sexuality?"

"When was it done?" my friend asked.

"It says 1935," I replied.

"A troubled time," he reflected. "The insect looks like a giant alien from the black outer space in the background of the picture. Hitler and Stalin were on the move destroying old certainties. Holland, the artist's country, was soon to be invaded.

"The church used to use insects in exorcisms in the Middle Ages," I said. "In Bushman mythology, the mantis is an important god of creation, Kaggen".

I was casting around for something to get hold of.

His final comments astonished me. "I think,' he said, "that you have to go to the work of Chuang Tzu. He dreamt he was a butterfly flying freely in the air. In the dream he has no idea that he is Chuang Tzu. Did the butterfly ask existential questions? Just by asking such questions in this way Chuang Tzu experienced spiritual freedom."

"How did you know that?" I asked, trying not to sound surprised.

"I found a book on Chaung Tzu in a second hand bookshop in Hong Kong," he replied.

A couple started giggling behind us. They had been listening to us.

"Honey, how come there's only one ticket booked for the honeymoon?" he said to her.

She spluttered with laughter.

"My third husband was such a nice flavour," she replied in a loud stage whisper.

"Listen, it's better if we just stay friends," he said barely able to contain himself.

"The honeymoon is over and I am still hungry," came her riposte.

I nodded to my friend that it was time to go. He nodded

back.

*Google M. C. Escher's 'Dream'.

The Snake Lady of Nakasero

This is not a pretty story. I thought long and hard before committing it to print. It concerns a man, a woman I call 'The Snake Lady' and knowledge that was, for a while, out of reach. Where shall I start? Perhaps in the City Bar, where so many other things began.

He would sit there in the afternoons, day after day. He was 'here'. Beyond the balustrade was 'there', 'The Other'. He rarely ventured out into it. He wanted to. It was just that he was too comfortable where he was and 'The Other' was too much like an open-air zoo for his liking.

He wrote this in his diary:

The Other

There was a magical world out there. We knew it was there, beyond the balcony wall of the City Bar in Kampala. It's just that many of us didn't want to know it. We knew we were surrounded by unknown knowns as well as known unknowns. We didn't want to know, for example, about the talking cockerel of Misindye village. We didn't really want to hear it say, in Luganda, that anyone who killed it and ate its flesh would surely die. We didn't want to know about animals possessed by evil spirits. "Not today, tomorrow perhaps," we would say. We preferred to allow a sepia screen, like a comforting veil of bark cloth, descend around us. Inside our cell we knew what we knew, which wasn't much at all.

"I think I'll stay here," he said to himself. He would order another Tusker.

A sense of wellbeing, of being in the most comfortable of

comfort zones, swept over him. At the same time, however, feelings of guilt nibbled like termites at the timbers of his complacency.

Nearly everybody at Bat Valley was writing a book or wanted to. He was no exception. As a student at the university he had formed a plan: to study the oral tradition in Uganda, to record it before it died out. The plan was elaborated in the City Bar in the presence of a colleague from Scotland who had worked as a busker in the Paris Métro. He needed his friend Maurice's input. Maurice was a folk-singer. He was the courageous one. John, by contrast, was nervous, apprehensive of venturing out into the Ugandan countryside.

At the time he couldn't understand himself. Why was he so hesitant about going into the bush? It took him some years to realise that it was because of a deep-seated fear of snakes. His father had shown black and white films at his birthday parties. One of them showed a man wrestling with a gigantic snake. His favourite childhood board game of Snakes and Ladders failed to dislodge the fear that had been implanted.

Eventually his contract came to an end. There had been an upsetting separation from his girlfriend. She had asked him to write to her as soon as he landed in Europe. He sent her a card from Greece. On it he wrote, "I was amazed to see Europeans working on the dust carts, the garbage carts, in Athens."

Why did he write that? He knew that it would annoy her. Was he trying to say, "It's over"?

Back in London, he took up a post in Barnet, lecturing in English. He began to experience regrets and pricks of conscience. The dismal flat he had rented from a friend who was still in Africa plunged him into deep gloom. He began to thirst for the sun, for Mary and for the project he had abandoned.

He set about asking himself why he didn't want to go back. One of his students produced photographs in class of huge snakes. He kept snakes as pets in his bedroom, he said. John felt sick. Then it dawned on him.

"Snakes! It is not Mary. It's snakes I am afraid of!" he said to himself as he was driving back to his flat in Finchley in his blue Ford Popular.

That is how it happened. He decided to go back to Buganda a) to overcome his fear of snakes and b) to fulfil his earlier dream of rescuing the stories of a disappearing oral tradition. He felt he owed it to Uganda.

He had studied the oral tradition in Ireland and had sent the script to publishers who had been making very positive noises. If he could get another major project under his belt, who knows where it would lead? He could become a major world figure. It was time now to come up with the goods.

The essence, the main plank of his plan was going to be The Snake in Ugandan Oral Story-Telling. Around this he planned to build archives on the tortoise, the crocodile, the buffalo and so on. The sub-categories would fall naturally into place.

He caught a taxi back to his old flat. Mary was still there. On the surface she appeared to be delighted to see him. His things were still there. The exquisitely carved Rwandan chairs were in their normal place by the door. He was glad to be back.

He and Mary sat down to talk. He explained to her that he wanted to revive his oral tradition project. Her response took his breath away:

"Oh, haven't you finished that yet?"

In his mind he had barely started, if at all.

"My idea is to go round primary schools in Buganda. Children love stories. I'll get them to tell me."

"They'll just be repeating what they have read in their books," Mary replied. "You know, Rosetta Baskerville's *The King of Snakes* sort of thing."

John was alarmed at Mary's lack of enthusiasm. He decided not to respond. He had just heard that the English Department at Bat Valley had offered him full use of the university's facilities At least *they* liked his proposal. They had even signalled that there could be an honorary doctorate in it for him.

He needed to face his phobia head-on. He had a phone call

from a friend who lived outside Kampala: a massive snake had been seen on the road. Borrowing Mary's car, he sped over to the spot where he thought it was. As he came round a corner, he saw the snake lying across the road, its head in the undergrowth on one side, its tail in the trees on the other. He didn't have time to stop. With a bump he drove straight over it.

Back in his old haunt, the City Bar, he ordered a cold lager to calm his nerves. He was delighted to see that some of his old mates were still there. He told them about the snake.

"It must have been a rock python," he said, on his third pint. "Huge thing. As I went over it, it clamped itself around the car, trying to wrestle it over. I kept driving, swerving this way and that, until, exhausted, it fell away."

The truth was that the snake was already dead when he ran over it. Curiously though, John felt good after he had told his tall story. He had a bounce in his step as he went back to Mary's car.

He began his research by visiting a school in Mukono. They were expecting him. He sat down with his tape-recorder. The children were on the floor already, in a circle. The teacher smiled and nodded. She began:

"'An old lady was walking through the village when she saw some people attacking a poisonous snake. She pushed them away and carried the snake back to her hut, where she tended its wounds. A close friendship grew up between them. One day they decided to go to Kampala. The lady picked the snake up and it bit her.'"

"I am dying, I am dying, I am dying!" she screamed.

"Why did you bite me? I am your friend. I saved your life! I trusted you!"

The snake looked up at her and said, "Madam, you knew I was a snake when you first picked me up."

"What does the story tell us?" Miss Mugamba asked.

"Never trust a snake," the children called out.

John turned the story over in his head as he drove back to Kampala. He felt both satisfied and, strangely, slightly troubled.

He went to the university library and jotted down stories from newspapers: 'Ugandan Woman Changes into a Snake', 'A Snake Swallows a Man in Mbarara'. Doubts began to surface. Was he on the right track?

He pushed the papers away and got up to look along the shelves. There was a book on Kintu. It argued that the 'Ethiopian' founder of the Baganda decapitated a snake at the beginning of the kingdom. "Must have been a metaphor for a rival tribe," John thought, although he was troubled by the similarity between Kintu, Nambi, Kintu's wife and Bemba, the snake, with the Bible's Adam and Eve and their snake. He noted that Bemba's country was already called Buganda. He still felt troubled inside.

He took down 'The Snake of the Baskervilles', as he jokingly called it, Rosetta Baskerville's book. The photocopier was out of order. It was comforting simply to jot down the familiar tale. He loved the way Waswa, in the story, conned the snake into getting into a water-pot, putting the lid on before it was put on a bonfire.

In spite of these early problems, John's research began to go well. He penetrated deeper and deeper into the countryside of Buganda. His collection of tapes grew and grew. He was becoming near-fluent in Luganda.

In the meantime, Mary became increasingly negative, even hostile to John's research. She was not from Buganda. She was from the north. Her family, including her uncle the President, were not happy about her relationship with John.

"You are never at home," she would complain when he came in. It was true. John was becoming obsessed with his snake stories.

One night he got back very late. There was a curfew on. There were soldiers on the road outside the flat on top of Nakasero Hill. They had said on television that anyone out after ten would be shot. It was five to ten. The streetlights were out. There was just a thin crescent moon. Then he saw it, curled up, on the top step by the door: the snake.

90

He heard a rifle being cocked. What was it to be, the soldiers or the snake? Would they shoot? They won't kill me, they will kill me. Are they from the north? Shall I call out, tell them who I am? Do they speak Swahili, Luganda, English, or something else, like Lugbara?

A snake bite could be fatal. Key in hand he jumped over the snake and put it in the lock. It wouldn't turn. He saw Mary looking at him through the glass door. Her face was expressionless. He felt a bite on his leg. Then he felt nothing.

The Spider Man of Gulu

Y ou probably won't know what to make of this story. It is, I admit, odd. Does it have a moral? I think it does but I'll leave it to you to work out.

She was a strange girl. Her father had a flourmill on the side of the Thames to the east of London. He also owned a major UK newspaper.

I met her in Africa. She didn't seem to like 'Europeans', even though she was one herself. I couldn't get to the bottom of it. She surrounded herself mainly with African politicians and academics.

She even had an unofficial 'bodyguard', an African-American poet, who took it upon himself to be the gatekeeper at her parties. If your face didn't fit, he would literally put out his arm to stop you going in. He did this with a smile that was friendly but also sinister. This was galling because she was a neighbour and a close friend of a close African friend of mine but that's by the by.

I couldn't work it out. Anyway, I came to terms with it. It takes all types. Rumour had it that she was up to her neck in something. I didn't believe it.

I knew that she had a problem: she was an acute arachnophobe.

Her parents had a small mansion that they used as a weekend retreat in St Albans. It was situated next to a former silk mill down by the river in the park. The factory went bust some time after the war. That's when they bought the house.

Now, St Albans has the reputation of being the 'City of Spiders'. They are everywhere, especially down by the Ver. Goodness knows when they came in. Some blame the Romans, others the Normans. Some say they are left over from the silk mill days. They say that certain spiders produced a silky thread that was used by the mill owner. I don't know. All I know is that Kate, Kate Lyle, kept her bedroom windows tightly shut to prevent 'unwelcome guests' from getting in.

She was literally terrified of the critters. Things came to a head when she was sanding the floor of the loft in the huge barn that she was converting into a studio for her art work. The barn had originally been the stables. A spider with a body the size of a mouse ran across in front of her. Her screams could be heard in the garden of The Fighting Cocks pub on nearby Abbey Mill Lane.

Kate's parents realised that something had to be done. A doctor had told them that it may have had something to do with her mother's extreme possessiveness. Another said that a fear of spiders could be linked to an anxiety about getting pregnant.

Both of her parents were neurotic about Kate's boyfriends, suspecting all of them of being gold-diggers. She was simply not allowed to develop a normal relationship with boys of her own or of any other background. Her father was behind this overprotectiveness - he had nieces who had been bitten badly by fortune hunters - but he left it to his wife to quiz Kate on whom she was seeing. This she did constantly.

Over dinner one day, a guest was telling the family that he had spent years in Uganda and had not seen a single spider. He had a theory that they must have been heavily predated. Mr Lyle wondered if the spiders of St Albans were under-predated. There are simply no predators in St Albans - no geckos, no chameleons, no snakes to hoover them up. Only a few bats.

On the spur of the moment, Kate sat up and said, "That's it. I want to go and live in that country, a place where there are no spiders!"

Reluctantly her parents agreed, her father pulled a few strings and, lo and behold, Kate received a letter asking her to join the Art Department at Bat Valley. Behind the scenes her father had oiled the wheels by secretly donating a huge sum of money to the university.

It had been decided that Kate had to face down her demons. Her father had rung the head of Art saying that he felt it could be good for Kate if she tackled her phobia head on. Could she be encouraged to create giant spiders out of *papier maché* or something like that? The department went one better. With their coffers overflowing, they approached the department of Artificial Intelligence with an idea for a joint project. The head of AI agreed.

Kate took up her post. It involved almost no contact with students. She was classed as a researcher. Under Dr Opio's supervision she set about creating robotic spiders. She called them 'spibots'.

She studied photographs of coconut spiders. Some were as big as a dog. Her first creation had a battery in it that was operated by a hand-held remote. She got the idea from her younger brother's remote control beach buggy. She herself had loved playing with it in the car park on the seafront in Port Eynon where her family owned a huge seaside house.

She would often be seen taking her 'coco-spibot' for walks around the roads of the university. As you can imagine, it caused a sensation. Kate enjoyed the attention.

She went on to bigger things. She found out that gigantic spiders had once, in the nineteenth century, been reported as living on the edge of Lake Victoria. There were astonishing tales about their vast nets.

She had heard rumours that much bigger spiders could be found in the Congo. She studied everything she could lay her hands on about them. She absorbed as much data as she could, including arguments against the possibility of such creatures having ever existed: the larger a spider gets, the heavier its exoskeleton becomes, rendering the animal incapable of movement. Nevertheless, she found the reports convincing. They hadn't been seen recently, she said, because they had retreated further into the forest, escaping from Man.

Her inventions became bigger and bigger. Eventually, after an awkward incident with a soldier in the city centre, she was asked by Dr Opio to take her 'spibots' for walks in the university's football stadium when it wasn't being used. This she did.

Kate was beginning to feel more positive towards spiders. She felt she was overcoming her phobia at last. The 'treatment', she believed, was working.

She told the pro-vice chancellor. He beamed. She asked if she could create huge spider statues, in the style of Louise Bourgeois, and display them around the grounds. He agreed. After all, she represented an income stream. Her creations were becoming famous and, on balance, as talking points they enhanced the university's profile. Bat Valley joined the Tourist Trail.

Fired by this success, Kate went one step further. She wanted to make a spider that would climb over a building. It was agreed. The day of the launch arrived. Guests were seated in rows in front of the main building. Kate pressed the button. An enormous spider appeared on the roof. It began to climb down the facade of the building. There were screams. Chairs were overturned. People scattered in every direction at the fearful sight. Kate was called in.

She was told that she had 'cool it' for a while. She didn't mind. The therapy had apparently worked. She felt that she had overcome her arachnophobia, despite the fact that she had not confronted a real spider once during her time in Kampala, either on campus or in and around her flat on Nakasero Hill. She emailed her parents to tell them she thought she was better and that she was going to take a holiday.

Now, her brother had worked on an aid programme in Uganda and had formed a network of friends dotted around the country. The custom was that you could just turn up, out of the blue, at anybody's house and expect to be put up and wined and dined. He told her he thought it was good that she was going to take a break.

He suggested that she visit a friend of his in Gulu. It was a long way from Kampala. Privately he felt it would be a good test for his sister. He had stayed with Peter himself and had had quite an experience.

Kate set off in her Saab. The car ate up the miles. It was getting dark when she arrived at Peter's house in a remote area outside Gulu. Owls were hooting. Crickets were chattering. He politely asked her in. Jokingly he recited some words from Mary Howitt's poem 'The Spider and the Fly':

"Will you walk into my parlour?" said the Spider to the Fly,
'Tis the prettiest little parlour that ever you did spy;
The way into my parlour is up a winding stair,
And I've a many curious things to shew when you are there."

Kate knew the poem well. She replied with a laugh:

"Oh no, no," said the little Fly, "to ask me is in vain,
For who goes up your winding stair can ne'er come down again."

Peter, Peter Southwood, had lived in Uganda for years. He was single. He had prepared a meal for her, a curry with delicious fruit side dishes. She was very grateful but began to have odd feelings about Peter. He wore thick-lensed glasses that exaggerated the size of his eyes. It gave the impression he was staring at her, without blinking. For a fleeting moment, they reminded Kate of the two prominent, glistening beady eyes of the six-eyed Jumping Spider. She dismissed the thought as a throw-back to the condition she had overcome.

"I'll show you to your room now," Peter said. He led Kate across to the other side of his bungalow.

"I'll leave you to it," he said, opening the door but not going in.

Kate went in. She was so tired she simply collapsed on the bed fully clothed. She was too tired to undress. She lay there enjoying the feeling of sleep coming over her. She sat up with a start.

"What was that?" she whispered.

She could hear tiny noises. Slowly she turned her eyes to the area around the bed. Dozens of spiders were leaping up and down all around the bed, some reaching tremendous heights. The shock was so great she passed out.

The following morning, Peter entered the room. He went over to the bed and closed Kate's eyes. He placed a sheet over her, covering her head.

"Joshua!" he called. Joshua was the ageing gentleman who had prepared the curry. He had worked for Peter for many years.

"Joshua! Fetch the trolley."

The Congolese Warthog Man

Moïse is a changed man. He saw the light one day when he was out hunting. This is what happened.

He would disappear into the jungle or the bush for weeks at a time. He was hunting warthog. Now you may think that this is a strange thing to do. Well, one can eat warthog. It is popular in Kampala. It tastes, unsurprisingly, of pork, but is stronger. At least, that is what I have been told.

In other words Moïse had a small business selling warthog meat. He ran it from a small stall in Owino market. The business was prospering. He had a fine house outside the city with a smallholding attached.

However, Moïse was not just a butcher. He had another string to his bow. He was an ivory carver. As you know, ivory comes not only from elephants. The tusks of walruses, hippopotami, some whales like the narwhal, and the remains of mammoths are also sources of the valuable material, as are the tusks of warthogs.

He was very proud of his carvings. He made all sorts of things: napkin rings, small boxes, even bishop's croziers, if he had a piece of tusk large enough. His ornaments for the house were exquisite. He would carve animals in the 'about to pounce' pose, snakes, crocodiles, monkeys, fish, even imitations of a warthog's head with tusks.

The trade in elephant ivory was being clamped down on. Both the Ugandan and the Kenyan governments had banned it and were fining poachers. They were burning whatever they could confiscate. Efforts were being made to get Tanzania to fall in line. The situation in the DRC was still chaotic.

Moïse is a gentle man. He doesn't like to break the law. It is legal to export, import, own or sell warthog teeth and tusks.

Warthogs are not an endangered species. Neither are boars or hippos. He sticks to the ivory of the warthog.

And so his life went on. His products were in high demand in Kampala's gift shops. The demand from tourists passing through Entebbe airport was insatiable. The Chinese loved his work. To vary the work of his sculptors, he encouraged his men and women to go out onto the streets and set up displays near expensive hotels and restaurants.

This side of his business was under threat. The cabinet had just ruled that street vendors should be banned from the streets of Kampala. Unpleasant scenes were occurring with some law enforcement officials ending up in hospital. The argument was that illegal traders were harming the businesses of those shopkeepers who were operating legally. Moïse was not worried. He had plenty of outlets, both official and unofficial.

However, he is now a changed man. He no longer hunts warthog. He had what he felt was a religious experience, an awakening, an epiphany. It was as if a guardian angel had intervened in his life.

He was out hunting warthogs near the Congo River. Moïse didn't mind travelling vast distances to catch his prey. He was originally from Katanga, a province of the Congo, the DRC, as it is now called. The DRC was like a second home to him. He speaks French fluently as well as several Congolese languages.

He was sitting at the edge of a track when he heard a commotion in the bushes nearby. He raised his gun ready to bag what sounded like a good-sized warthog. He had established that they were in the vicinity by examining fresh hoof marks in the mud. He lined up his eye with the sight at the end of the barrel.

A lion appeared. It crouched down and started growling. He was heard to say 'merde' quite loudly - 'sugar' in polite English.

The lion got ready to attack. Moïse was shaking like a leaf. He was sure he was going to miss. The lion began to creep closer. Moïse said his prayers. He promised to change his ways. He was sure, though, that he was a dead man.

Suddenly a warthog emerged from some tall grass and rushed down the track that separated him from the lion. The lion sprang after the hog and disappeared after it into the trees. Moïse fainted.

Since that day, Moïse has not killed a single warthog. The full impact, the horror of his treatment of warthogs, had hit him like a hammer. All of his souvenirs, keepsakes and ornaments are made now from hippo teeth.

He tells me that it was bound to be like that. That, as a child, his tribe had used small bags of fragmented warthog tusk in ceremonies linked to establishing contact with the gods. He had seen the light. For him the warthog was now something special, a creature to be revered. It had returned to having the religious significance it had had for him when he was a child in Mpungu.

He took to keeping wounded warthogs on his small farm. He looked after them and paid vets to treat them. His wife was slightly put out by this new pattern of behaviour. Their income had gone down and they had school fees to pay. Moïse was becoming really fond, over-fond, his wife claimed, of a hog he had christened 'Donald'.

"You care more about that pig than you do about me," she would say. Moïse paid no attention.

They say that he can be seen now driving around Kampala in an old Ford Fiesta with his favourite warthog sitting by his side. He takes Donald with him everywhere. They say that he is not only neglecting his wife and children, his business is going downhill too.

He was stopped by a policeman recently who asked him what he was doing with a warthog in his car.

"That hog needs to be in a zoo," the policeman said. Moïse smiled with that infectious smile of his. The policeman smiled and waved him on. He had seen worse things. He often stops men with goats on the back of the bicycles.

A week later he was stopped again.

"I thought I said take him to Entebbe zoo," the policeman complained.

"I did," Moïse answered. "It was great. Donald really enjoyed it. Today we are off to the beach in Entebbe."

The warthog nodded and grinned, baring his tusks. Yes indeed, Moïse is a changed man.

Bat Valley

Eli Berg was a chiropterologist, an expert on bats. His interest in bats in Africa had first been fired by a reference in a book to the straw-coloured fruit megabats, Latin name *Eidolon helvum*, that populated the eucalyptus trees along Kampala Road. His ambition, his dream, was to establish a chair of Chiropterology for himself at Bat Valley University.

He couldn't put his finger on exactly why the sight and sound of bats on Kampala Road had inspired him. Was it the fact that they took to the sky each day at a given moment with a precision that you could almost set your watch by? Was it the strange whistling sound, like rustling tin foil, that they made as they took off into the darkening sky? Was it the slight shiver of dread that the sight of the black cloud gave him? Was it their restless movement in the trees and their chattering during the day? Was it the fact that the bats seemed so intent on getting somewhere but few knew where that was? Some said they went to the Ssese Isles at night but others said they flew down to Zambia to gorge on mangoes. How long would it have taken them to get there and back? Questions like this about the Wandegeya bats often occupied his thoughts.

Batman comics, together with those with Superman in them, had been his favourite reading as child. He had wanted to be like Batman or, at least, Robin. Batman was human. Superman was an alien from the planet Krypton. He identified more with Batman, even though the latter only did his good deeds at night and was dependent upon gadgets rather than Superman's superhuman power.

His family had taken refuge from Nazi Germany in 1933, moving into a house halfway up the steep hill in Port Eynon, on the Gower Peninsula, near Swansea. It was there that he heard old Gower people say that the moths that came out at night were really witches. He hadn't liked to hear that.

It had also troubled him when he heard the older generation making nasty references to bats. He had heard old women in the family kitchen mutter that a certain woman in the village was a witch who could turn into a crow, a raven, a moth or a bat at night.

His research at Swansea University, to which he was appointed after gaining his first degree at University College, London, had taken him to the Americas to study the bat-shaped, dark-coloured, nocturnal Black Witch, the *Ascalapha odorata*, a moth held to herald death in Mexico and the Caribbean. He noted the overlap between bats and moths in the superstitious mind. Bats and moths – he was torn between the two. Which way should he go?

It was the bat, the beloved *reremouse* of his childhood in Gower, that eventually began to consume him. He loved the word. He discovered that the plural was *reremice* and that the word came from the Middle English *reremous*, and before that from the Old English term for a bat: *hrēremūs* or *hrērmūs*. He realised that, as could be seen from the variants *rearmouse* and *reermouse*, the first part of the word meant to rear, from the Old English *hrēran* – to move, to shake, to stir. Bats rear up to avoid you, he thought. He filled his lectures at BVU like this, with references to the etymology and the English dialect words of flora and fauna, much to the dismay of his students who felt they were being given useless and irrelevant knowledge.

As a teenager he had toured nearby parts of Wales and England on his Claude Butler bicycle, collecting the dialect names for a bat: bellybat, ink-mouse, leathern-bat, rat-bat, billy-bat, ekkymowl, flitter-mouse – the list went on and on. He adored the sound, the feel even, of these words. During a holiday in Scotland he had heard the words *backe* and *bakie* bird to describe a bat.

He loved the German word *die Fledermaus*. Passing his

house on the road that climbs the hill and leads out of Port Eynon, locals would marvel at the sound, emerging from his bedroom window, of Johann Strauss II's opera *Die Fledermaus, The Revenge of the Bat*, as it sometimes called, played on his old wind-up gramophone.

The notes he took with him to Bat Valley University (his second post) filled a whole trunk. It contained a box of posters with such snippets on them as:

> A bat flying around your house three times is a death omen.
> A bat flying into a barn or a house means it's going to rain.
> It is unlucky to see a bat during daylight.
> Killing a bat can shorten your life.
> It's lucky to keep a bat bone somewhere in your clothes.
> Keeping the right eye of a bat in your waistcoat pocket will make you invisible.
> Carrying powdered bat heart in your pocket will prevent a man from bleeding to death and can stop a bullet.
> Washing your face in the blood of a bat helps you to see in the dark.
> Slipping a few drops of bats' blood into a person's drink makes him or her more passionate.

He had pinned these up on the walls of his office in Kampala. The Dean had asked him to remove them but Eli explained that his intention was partly humorous and partly an attempt to get students to reflect on the stupidity of superstition. The posters stayed put.

He had dozens of books and articles on bats in that trunk. He even collected popular poems about bats with which he regaled his students. There was a Cornish one he chanted in his lectures, whilst strumming his guitar. It was sung, he argued, to avoid bad luck on seeing a bat:

Airy mouse, airy mouse, fly over my head.
And you shall have a crust of bread
And when I brew and when I bake,
You shall have a piece of my wedding cake.

Curiously, the students quite liked the way he quoted Shakespeare on bats. At the end of lectures he would often say, "On the bat's back I do fly", referring to Ariel's steed in *The Tempest*. "Some war with rere-mice for their leathern wings, / To make my small elves coats" (Titania in *A Midsummer's Night Dream)* was frequently quoted by Eli, as well as "the wool of bat" that goes into the witches' cauldron in *Macbeth*.

The authorities at Bat Valley became alarmed at the direction Eli's research was going. Complaints were landing on the Dean of the Faculty of Natural Science's desk with troubling regularity. "Berg's lectures are rubbish" was a common one.

He was also beginning to act unwisely. For example, he would often venture out after dark - and after curfew - to visit his bat traps dotted around the campus. The army did not bother to patrol the university grounds – officers used to use the college bar - so a blind eye was turned to Eli's nocturnal wanderings.

A mock voodoo session in his flat, involving West African bat-gods and Nigerian students, had been mischievously reported in the student newspaper, *The Campus Bee*. He had pleaded with his Dean that it was just academic research.

He had fallen into a swamp one night when he was out on a bat hunt and had almost been caught by a crocodile. The wooden dugout canoe in which he had set off turned turtle and it was a miracle that he managed to squeeze his rather fat waist out of it and swim unscathed to join his frantic wife who was waiting anxiously for him on dry land. The canoe he had hired disappeared and the university was asked to stump up to meet the cost of a new one.

He had, in fact, often wandered unwisely into Lake Victoria at night and had caught some disease, which kept him in bed for quite a while. It couldn't have been bilharzia because that would not have had any obvious effects for some years. It was all a bit of a mystery. Colleagues had not been best pleased at having to cover his lectures for him.

He had got into a fight with a street-vendor who was selling bat-meat, considered a delicacy by some in Uganda. The case had almost gone to trial but the plaintiff opted for a very substantial out-of-court settlement.

He had almost come a cropper when investigating an alleged witch who claimed she could recruit bats and snakes to do her evil bidding. Villagers had turned on him and given him a beating when they realised that he may have been trying to rubbish her work. Eli was slowly becoming a liability. His job, in fact, was on the line. To cap it all, he began to feel that he was being plagued by bad luck.

Concern was raised that he had been spending far too much time on a bat centre for tourists in Entebbe. The project was failing. Questions were being raised at Vice-Chancellor level about Eli's Bat World. The University was beginning to feel that the venture, initially viewed as a possible money-spinner, was not, after all, worth supporting. Tourism had taken a dip because of a political flair-up in the country, a power struggle between rival tribes. Shots could be heard at night coming from the town centre.

Eli was oblivious to anything like that. He loved his stuffed bats. He would spend hours walking from cabinet to cabinet in the Entebbe centre admiring his vast collection, the work of half a lifetime: the Mindanao Pygmy Fruit Bat, Brooks's Dayak Fruit Bat, Franket's Epauletted Bat, the Demonic Tube-Nosed Bat, the Bougainville Monkey-Faced Bat, the Angolan Rousette, the Moss-Forest Blossom Bat, The Ethiopean Woolly Bat, the Hoary Wattled Bat, Curry's Bat, the Botswana Long-Eared Bat, Moloney's Flat-Headed Bat, the Azores Noctule, the Dar es Salaam Pipistrelle, the Greater Hairy-Winged Bat, the Equatorial Dog-Faced Bat, the Peter Wrinkle-Lipped Bat, the Shaggy Bat, the Naked-Rumped Pouched Bat, the Egyptian

Tomb Bat, the Large-Eared Horseshoe Bat, the Antillean Ghost-Faced Bat and the Hairy-Legged Vampire Bat, to mention but a few.

He had at one point explored the possibility that dead bats could be good for you. A friend of his was teaching at a school in Tororo, a town near the Uganda-Kenya border. They had often discussed Eli's bat research interests over beers on the terrace of the Rock Hotel. This friend had called him to say that he had noticed a funny taste in the tap water in his house on the school compound. He had gone up into the roof and discovered that the tank was full of rotting bats! Roy, his friend, had disinfected the system with Dettol. The thing that had astonished Roy was that he had not had a bad stomach, even though he had been drinking water laced with putrified bat. The University financed a small research project proposed by Eli into the possible benefits to health of dead bat flesh but results were inconclusive.

A paper he had given in Dar es Salaam saw him hanging on to his post by the skin of his teeth. In it he reviewed - expertly, it was generally admitted - the literature concerning the spread of Ebola. Originally, he argued, it was thought to have been spread by the eating of gorilla meat. Now, he concluded sadly, humans seemed to be catching the disease from bats. Apes and humans contract it, he reported, from eating food that bats have drooled over or defecated on, or by coming into contact with surfaces covered in infected bat droppings and then touching their eyes or mouth with their fingers.

One day at dusk, standing on the treeless side of Kampala Road - 'Bat Valley' was his favourite place in the city - he was gazing up at the huge colony of bats taking off into the night sky. His wife Luna had often stood there with him holding the machine with which he measured pollution levels. He was exploring the theory that an increase in traffic fumes was causing a drop in bat numbers. The road where they rested during the day channelled traffic coming from the north of the country through the valley below Bat Valley University.

Anyway, on that particular day he was almost in a trance, mesmerised by the sight of the rising army of bats. He found himself being drawn closer and closer to the dark cloud, as if a vacuum was being created by their energy and he was being sucked into it. He felt that his soul was flying out of him, upwards into the black swarm.

He woke up in Mulago hospital to find his wife Luna sitting next to him.

"Eli, you stepped in front of one of those motorcycle taxis - what are they called? - a *boda-boda*. You are lucky to be alive."

He slipped back into a coma. Luna Berg was by his beside when he next came round. He beckoned to her to come closer.

"Luna," he said, - Luna, the name of a moth, was the pet-name he had given her - "Luna, my little moth, you have stuck with me through thick and thin. When I was almost fired from the University over that bat-meat incident, you stood by me."

"Yes, my dear," Luna said.

"Even now, as my Bat World project is folding, you are here by my side."

"Of course, my darling."

"When I got shot that night bat-hunting on Kampala Golf Course, after the curfew hour, you nursed me back to health."

"Yes, dear."

"You know, dear Luna, what I think?"

"What, my love?" she whispered.

"You're a blooming jinx!"

Notes

'The Jaguar Man of Kiziba' was first published in Spanish as 'El Jaguar del último rey de Ruanda' in one of the *Siete pecados* (Seven Deadly Sins) short story anthologies, *Envidia,* edición a cargo de Susana Furphy Arroyo, Benma grupo editorial, Mexico, 2014.

The 'Praying Mantis Man' is adapted from a story first published in my book *A Night in Buganda, Tales from Post-Colonial Africa,* Verulamium Press, St Albans (2014). http://robertgurney.com/anightinbuganda/

By the same author:

La poesía de Juan Larrea, Universidad del País Vasco, Lejona, 1985

Poemas a la Patagonia, Verulamium Press, St Albans, 2004

Luton Poems, Verulamium Press, St Albans, 2005

Nueve monedas para el barquero, Verulamium Press, St Albans, 2005

El cuarto oscuro y otros poemas / The Dark Room and Other Poems, Lord Byron Ediciones, Madrid, 2008

Poemas a la Patagonia, edición aumentada, Lord Byron Ediciones, Madrid, 2009

La libélula y otros poemas / The Dragonfly and Other Poems, Lord Byron Ediciones, Madrid, 2012

La casa de empeño y otros poemas / The Pawn Shop and Other Poems, Lord Byron Ediciones, Madrid, 2014

A Night in Buganda, Tales from Post-Colonial Africa, Verulamium Press, St Albans, 2014

To Dylan, Cambria Books, Llandeilo, 2014

Dylan's Gower, Cambria Books, Llandeilo, 2014

El acantilado, Cambria Books, Llandeilo, 2014

Absurd Tales from Africa, Cambria Books, Llandeilo, 2017

Translation*: The River and Other Poems*, translation of Andrés Bohoslavsky's *El río y otros poemas*, Verulamium Press, St Albans, 2004

Reviews

Annie Davison (UK) on Robert's *Absurd Tales from Africa* (2017): "The beauty of these tales lies in the wonderful pictures created in my imagination. The humour arises when life goes wrong for people in serious situations, a bit like John Cleese in the immensely watchable Fawlty Towers."

Colin Townsend (Canada) on *A Night in Buganda* (2014): "An extraordinary book – unlike any other I have read ... stories brought together with a poet's flair for language ... they will have you laughing, crying or perhaps just wondering."

Niall Herriot (Ireland) on *A Night in Buganda*: "It's a brilliant piece of writing."

On *Absurd Tales from Africa*: "I enjoyed Absurd Tales, not only for the zany humour and the wildly imaginative scenarios but also how the characters and settings for the stories reminded me so vividly of those times."

www.ingramcontent.com/pod-product-compliance
Lightning Source LLC
Chambersburg PA
CBHW071327130626
46556CB00004B/1775